THE CAMINO CRYSTAL

An Ainsley Walker Gemstone Travel Mystery

J.A. JERNAY

ISBN (electronic): 978-1-960936-23-3

ISBN (print): 978-1-960936-24-0

SAN SEBASTIÁN

CHAPTER ONE

Though the sphalerite necklace appeared to be perfect, Ainsley Walker was determined to find a flaw.

Holding the loupe to her eye, she leaned over the counter, her eye roving the piece for irregularities. If she looked hard enough, she knew she could find one. All jewelry, no matter the manufacturer, carried imperfections.

It was her last day of vacation in San Sebastián, the famous resort city on the coast of northern Spain, and Ainsley had entered this boutique in search of a piece of jewelry to bring home. So far she hadn't found it. This one had seemed hopeful, since it catered to the well-heeled tourist. Aside from the jewelry, there was an array of other items on the glossy shelving to be sold—fans, trivets, ceramic bowls.

Reclining in an antique chair nearby was her boyfriend, Joaquim. He looked exquisitely bored.

"Look at this, baby," she said.

"Only if you're going to buy it," he replied.

"*Señorita?*" said Ainsley. She motioned to the solicitous

salesgirl standing nearby. The girl was anxiously cupping her hands.

"Yes?" she replied.

"I understand how hard it is to cut sphalerite," said Ainsley. "I mean, everybody knows that, right? It has six directions of cleavage. But do you see this? Look."

The girl bent down and looked through the loupe. "What do I see?"

"That angle. Near the pavé. It's a terrible cut."

The salesgirl set the loupe down. "I'm sorry."

"Now you can see why it's overpriced."

"I can't change the price."

Ainsley smiled nicely. "I don't want the piece. I just want you to see why—"

Joaquim cut in. "Give the girl a break, Ainsley."

She turned to him. "What's your problem?"

"She didn't make the necklace," he said, "so stop making her feel bad."

"But they have to know why the price isn't correct."

"There's no such thing as the perfect piece of jewelry."

"And this sure isn't it."

The salesgirl looked crushed. Ainsley instantly regretted the words, and she realized that she'd let her mouth go too far again.

"Is there anything else you were interested in?" the salesgirl said.

Joaquim stood up and sauntered over. He pointed at the shelving behind her. "I'd like to buy one of those hand fans."

"The *abanico de mano*?"

"Yes."

"It's for you?" said Ainsley.

He wrapped an arm around her. "No," he replied, "it's for you. Don't complain."

"Which one would you like?" said the salesgirl.

"The white one," he said.

The salesgirl nodded, selected the fan, and put it in a small bag. Joaquim paid for it with a credit card.

"Thank you," said the salesgirl, "and have a nice day."

Joaquim handed the bag to Ainsley. "Let's go outside, my princess."

CHAPTER TWO

She and Joaquim stepped out into the sunlight of a summer afternoon. It was the very beginning of tourist season here in Basque country, just over the Pyrenees from France, and the streets were crawling with people of all stripes all on holiday.

"Look," she said, stuffing the fan into her bag, "I am very picky about my jewelry, and if I am going to spend three hundred euros, it has to be *perfect*."

"I'm not disagreeing with you—"

"And I told you that I wanted to find an unusual piece to buy here. So I can remember this place."

He sighed. "You search for other people's gemstones for a living. Don't you need to take a break from them?"

"No, because gemstones are my passion."

"Try origami instead. At least it'll be cheaper."

They were strolling through La Parte Vieja, the most image-conscious portion of the city. The streets were laden with high-end shops and boutiques, and Ainsley tried not to notice the sunburned faces of well-heeled French tourists swarming the sidewalks with ice cream cones.

"I just want to find something that nobody else has," she said.

"Nobody else has that bracelet."

He was pointing at her wrist. Ainsley looked down. She was wearing an orange plastic bracelet that she'd bought last month for ninety-five dollars. It was meant to signify her support for some nebulous campaign of self-empowerment, but she'd already forgotten its meaning. The truth was that, for the first time, she'd been sucked into the awesome power of a trend. Everyone she knew back in the United States had begun wearing them.

"That's temporary," she said.

"Besides," continued Joaquim, "why do you need something that nobody else has? So you can brag?"

Ainsley was growing more defensive. "No, I just appreciate fine workmanship."

"You can appreciate fine workmanship without *purchasing* it."

She stared at her boyfriend. "Why are you so difficult?"

"That's funny—I was going to ask you the same thing."

A dark expression crossed Ainsley's face. "Tell me exactly how I am difficult."

Her boyfriend groped for the right words. She could tell he was trying to be diplomatic. "Well," he finally said, "you are very intent on decorating yourself beautifully. No matter what the price."

"So what are you saying?"

He fell silent.

"You think that I'm materialistic," she said.

"Ainsley—"

She stopped walking, grabbed Joaquim's arm, and swung him around to face her. "Yes, it's true—I value material things. I buy gemstones, clothing, shoes. That's just who I am." She poked him in the sternum with a finger. "It doesn't mean that I hate people."

"True," he said, "but there are times when that line gets a little blurry. Like what just happened in there."

"That jewelry was crap. You know it, I know it—"

"Yes, but you didn't need to tell the poor girl that."

She pondered this. Slowly she became aware of the giant façade of a church behind her boyfriend. A sign read the San Maria del Coro Basilica. It was a gorgeous house of worship.

Joaquim followed her gaze and turned around. "I know what we're doing next. We're going to confession."

She snorted. "I haven't done anything wrong."

"That's debatable. But sometimes it's good just to talk to the priest."

"Forget it."

"Why?"

"Because I don't have to. That's a crazy idea."

"It's not any crazier than going to a shrink. Many priests are trained in psychology too."

Putting aside her feelings for a moment, Ainsley thought about it. Joaquim did make some sense. As science had begun to replace religion in the West, the psychologists had begun to replace the priests, and those suffering from moral or spiritual crises had turned from the kneeler to the couch. She remembered reading once that self-help books had been the best-selling genre of books in the United States, nearly a billion dollars of revenue per year.

Ainsley tried to imagine what a billion dollars looked like. She couldn't, not really, but she could imagine that it might help one's self quite a bit.

A roguish look passed across Joaquim's face. "Seriously," he said. "You can wait for me while I go to confession and talk about all the dirty thoughts I've had about you since I woke up this morning."

"Something tells me I'll be waiting a long time."

"And then," he said, "you go after me."

"But I'm not even Catholic—"

"It doesn't matter. Nobody checks for a rosary around your neck."

Ainsley looked at her boyfriend, feeling her heart torn between love and resentment. Joaquim always had bizarre ideas, and yet they often worked, so she had learned to simply go along with them. He truly marched to the beat of an unseen drummer.

"So that's really how you want to spend our last full day in San Sebastián?" she said.

"It'll take half an hour, at most."

Ainsley was confused. They'd spent the last week strolling the promenade, eating *pinxtos*, swimming at Ondarreta, making love, drinking *rioja*. Now Joaquim was insisting that they confess their sins.

"You're being weird," she said.

"Trust me." He offered his arm. "There's no reason for us to fight."

She glanced at his arm, then up to his face.

"If you insist," she said.

She laced her hand into the crook of his elbow, and together they began to walk towards the basilica.

CHAPTER THREE

As Ainsley entered the house of worship, her eyes roved the interior, taking in the design.

Apse, check. Nave, check. Transept, check.

It was a traditional Catholic design. Choir stalls, marble floors, good lighting. The air was thick with the scent of cleaning polish. The place was as modern as a basilica can be.

Joaquim was already sauntering down the middle of the nave, between the thick rounded pillars. He had a natural confidence. Ainsley followed behind, more slowly, wondering where the confession was going to happen.

Then she saw it.

Against the wall, in a darkened corner of the transept, stood a beautifully etched wooden box. It was about the size of a photo booth. There were two small doors, each decorated with a thick latticework. A small sign read

Padre Contrera
De 1300 a 1500 horas

She watched Joaquim knock on the door, wait for an

answer, then step inside. He drew the door shut behind him. The confessional was sturdy and didn't shake.

Ainsley sat down on a nearby chair, bare and wooden. Inside her mind, she felt the little scampering trickster known as Curiosity begin to wake up. What else did Joaquim want to confess to? Extortion? Grand larceny? A crisis of faith? Every perverted sexual thought under the sun? Or would he and the priest just chat like a couple of housewives leaning over a fence?

She tiptoed over to the box, held her breath, and listened. Inside the wooden confessional was the low sound of murmuring.

Then the door suddenly opened, knocking Ainsley down to the floor.

Joaquim looked down at her, an amused look on his face. "Little spoon," he said, "spying on me is pointless. I'll tell you whatever you want to know."

"What did you tell him?"

He lifted her to her feet. "I told him that the next girl was going to need a lot of help."

She punched Joaquim in the shoulder. "You're a dick."

"Watch the language," he said. "Padre Contrera doesn't much care for westernized women and their sailors' tongues."

"You and Padre Contrera seem to have grown very close," she said.

"Yeah, we go way back. About five minutes."

He held the door open for Ainsley. She ducked her head and stepped into the confessional.

Then she stuck her head back out and lowered her voice and cupped her mouth. "What do I *say*?"

"Nothing. Just listen to his advice."

Ainsley closed the door. A kneeler waited, facing a small window to the priest. She got down on her knees. It was surprisingly plush, two deep indents formed by the embarrassed knees of many previous sinners.

The small window flipped open. Ainsley jerked back a little, startled. Then she was looking at a screen, and on the other side of the screen, close enough to hear his breathing, was the bowed head of an old priest. He was facing sideways, and in the dim lighting, Ainsley was able to make out only the barest of profiles—a fleshy chin, a rounded nose, protuberant lips. His gray hair was clipped short and he wore a Roman collar.

Without turning his head, Padre Contrera said in a very low voice, "Good afternoon, my child."

"Hello," she replied.

"Are you nervous, my child?"

She grew annoyed at the diminutive. "I'm not a child and I'm not nervous." She drew herself up a little taller. "My name is Ainsley Walker."

"Tell me what you have to confess."

"Nothing."

"Then why have you come to see me?"

"My boyfriend told me that I should come in here to talk to you about my life."

"Did something happen to cause him to say this?"

She paused. "I was shopping for jewelry this afternoon and I kind of lost my temper."

He closed his eyes and inhaled deeply. "Most people begin by saying, *Forgive me, father, for I have sinned, it has been a week since my last confession.*"

"I haven't sinned," she replied, "I just lost my temper. And this is my first confession."

"You have no shortcomings to discuss?"

Ainsley thought about it. "None that I can think of."

The priest grimaced, as though he were in physical pain. "I want you to reflect upon that answer."

"Okay."

He fell silent. Ainsley shifted on her knees, feeling the stress in her lower back. Being a Catholic was hazardous to one's body—standing, kneeling, holding weird poses. It was like Italian yoga.

"What have you found?" he said.

"Nothing."

"Then continue reflecting."

Ainsley began to think about all the misfortune in her life. She'd been married once, to a man known only as the Legal Weasel, and supported him through his mess of a law school education. Soon after graduation, she'd come home to a half-empty apartment. He'd slipped right out of their home under the cloak of darkness.

Not her fault.

There was her spotty work history. Over the last decade, she had worked as a receptionist, waitress, landscaper, secret shopper, warehouse shipping clerk, bookstore clerk, publisher's assistant, magazine researcher, and barista—and those were just the ones she wanted to remember. At least thirty different positions, by her count, until she'd found her niche as a gemstone detective. Was impatience with one's position in life a sin? No.

Again, not her fault.

Then she thought about her father. He'd taken her on a vacation each of the first eight years of her life. She had the foot photos to prove it. He'd snapped pictures of their four bare feet overlooking a cypress swamp in South Carolina, a canyon in New Mexico, a snowy mountain range in Alaska, a pine forest in Michigan. Then the little carcinogenic masses had formed in his liver, hospice had appeared in the living room, and one morning there had been a trip to a nearby lake with a ceramic urn. Ainsley still had those foot photos, had stared at them for years until she'd forgotten his face but memorized every detail of the tops of his feet.

Yet again, not her fault.

"Padre," she said, "many unfortunate things have happened to me, but they were all caused by other people or bad luck."

The priest cleared his throat and shifted. He cupped his chin with a hand. "Then you," he said, "are a perfect human being."

His tone wasn't sarcastic. He was simply stating a fact.

"That's not funny," she said.

"I wasn't making a joke," he replied. "Can I ask you a question?"

"Okay."

"What do you value most in this world?"

Ainsley thought hard. "Relationships with people."

"Is that true?"

"I think so."

"You don't value anything else?"

Ainsley was reminded of the conversation she'd just had with Joaquim. "Maybe jewelry."

He nodded sagely. "It's a common vice. How does jewelry make you feel?"

She lowered her head. "Like an important person."

"Interesting."

"I'm also an investigator. I help people find their gemstones."

"*Las piernas preciosas* carry much perceived value."

"Indeed."

"Do you own jewelry?"

"Yes."

"How much?"

"I don't know. I never had it appraised."

"You can't estimate?"

"Maybe twenty thousand dollars."

She was surprised to hear that figure blurt out of her mouth. She'd never admitted it to herself before, the fact that she'd essentially screwed herself financially for the next decade, blowing all of her discretionary income—and even more—on rings, bracelets, necklaces, earrings, and other pieces of filigreed and vintage loveliness. In fact, purchasing jewelry had been a full-fledged addiction for most of her adult life, and, like all junkies, Ainsley had gone to ludicrous lengths to keep getting her fix, to keep jamming that needle between her toes. Her monthly credit-card statements were her track marks. They were proof of the depth of the hole into which she'd dug herself.

But she couldn't resist its siren call. She dreamed of it, wanted it, needed it, lusted for it. It wasn't just something that she did for other people's money. Ainsley needed gemstones to feel complete.

"And did you buy any jewelry here in San Sebastián?" said the priest.

"No," she said, "I couldn't find anything that I liked."

There was a long silence from the other side of the screen. Ainsley could see that Padre Contrera's eyes were closed. He seemed to be in a state of deep meditation.

"I'm going to make a strange request, Miss Walker," he said, "but it has a purpose."

"Okay."

"I would like you to take a walk with me."

CHAPTER FOUR

Ainsley tilted her head, her mouth falling slightly open. She didn't have the foggiest clue what that could mean. But she'd always thrived on the unknown.

"Right now?"

"Yes," he said, "it's almost three o'clock anyways."

"Okay," she said.

They exited the confessional. Outside of the box, the priest was a nondescript Spanish man, about Ainsley's height, with rounded shoulders. He donned a pair of glasses that made him look even more like wallpaper.

"Follow me," he said.

He began to make a slow loop through the cathedral, his arms folded upon one another. Ainsley walked slowly alongside him. She looked over to Joaquim, who was waiting in a pew, and shrugged. He smiled back and checked his phone.

"Near this city," said the priest, "runs a very old path. It's called the Camino de Santiago."

"My boyfriend told me about it."

"It is a medieval pilgrimage route, taken by hundreds of thousands of people every year. They started in France and walked westward across the Pyrenees, across northern Spain, all the way to Galicia in the northwest part of the peninsula. There, in Santiago de Compostela, they ended their journey and received absolution. Many were very sick, looking for something to heal themselves."

She smiled politely. "That's a nice story."

"It is," he agreed. "I would like to tell you another story about the Camino. But it's a secret one."

Ainsley lifted her ears. "A secret? Why are you telling me a secret?"

"Because you seem like someone very special."

That tickled her fancy. There was nobody on earth who didn't like being called special.

"Then please continue."

His finger crooked. She edged in until her shoulder was nearly pressed flat alongside his.

"A long time ago," he said, "in the thirteenth century, there was a princess from Cantabria. She was asked to marry, against her will, to a prince of A Coruña, which is a region in the northwest. To entice her into the marriage, the princess's family commissioned a special tiara to be worn for her. It was made of crystal."

"A crystal tiara," said Ainsley.

"Yes."

"I'm listening."

"Good," said Padre Contrera, smiling. "As they marched her along the Camino, through the baking hot days and rainy cold nights, she refused to take off her beautiful prize. Then, one night, as the marriage party slept, the princess decided to escape. She crept out of the camp and placed her tiara in a secret hiding place. Then she walked to the edge of a mountain."

"And?"

"And she flung herself off the side."

Listening raptly, Ainsley had forgotten about everything else in the world. This was exactly the type of story that would get her imagination racing.

"Padre," she said, "why are you telling me this?"

"Because for centuries nobody knew where this tiara was located."

"And now?"

He lowered his voice until it was barely audible. "I have learned how to find it."

She felt her palms instantly moisten. "Tell me."

"A friend of mine, a professor, discovered a very old account of the event, stuffed into the binding of a book from the Spanish Renaissance. He translated it last month."

Ainsley's heart skipped one, two, then three beats. Her imagination went into hyperdrive. She'd always been confident in her abilities as a gemstone investigator, but typically she was working for other people. This priest was dangling the opportunity to search for a historic crystal tiara ***on her own***. The experience would be priceless. So could its value.

"My question," he said, "is simple. Do you want to know where it is?"

"I would," she answered.

"But there is a catch."

"What is it?"

"To find the tiara, you must walk the Camino."

"Why?"

"Because the translation doesn't offer the exact location. It only offers a metaphorical description of the landscape."

She clapped her hands together. "That's fine. I've navigated with worse. And I lose some weight anyways."

The priest turned his head and looked at her squarely in the face for the first time. His eyes were a pair of inscrutable black holes. "Are you sure you want to know?"

"Of course. How long is the Camino?"

The smallest of smirks lifted the corner of his mouth. "How far do you think?"

"Maybe thirty or forty kilometers."

"It's eight hundred kilometers."

Ainsley felt her stomach fall into her shoes. Eight hundred kilometers. That wasn't any ordinary walk. She did the math in her head. That was twenty marathons, back to back. It would take weeks, maybe even months.

They were passing directly in front of the altar, and Ainsley stopped. "You've been very sweet to tell me," she said, "but I don't want to walk the Camino, Padre."

"As you wish," he replied.

"I'm leaving tomorrow," she said, "and I have a life waiting for me back at home."

He nodded sagely. "Those are good reasons to turn it down."

She stared at the priest. Something about his tone was too agreeable. It felt as though he were yessing her to death.

"What are you trying to say?" she said.

The priest's dark eyes bore directly into hers. She felt herself drawn into them, gripped by a higher power.

"What," he said, "do you hear inside yourself?"

"It's saying something else," she admitted.

He smiled. "Miss Walker, think about it. If you change your mind, come back to see me. And if I'm not here, then get on your knees in that confessional and see if you can feel it again."

The priest winked at her, then moved away towards a hidden door in darkness at the corner of the apse. He slipped through it, the door closed, and he was gone.

Ainsley watched him go.

"That," she said, "was very weird."

CHAPTER FIVE

That evening, Ainsley read the small business card in her hand. It said *Gizon Handi*. She looked up at the door and saw the same words printed there.

This was a *txoko*, or an eating club, an institution in Basque country that echoed back to the turn of the last century, when men from the farmland moved into the city, and tried to preserve their rural ways by meeting in private kitchens for long nights of *txakoli*, the local white wine, and excellent cooking. The events had traditionally been all-male, but most of them had begun allowing women for the last few years.

Joaquim had learned about this place from a friend. It didn't advertise, didn't have a web presence, didn't do anything, apparently, except make its attendees feel superior to the eight billion other people in the world who would never taste these men's cooking. In fact, Ainsley thought the word *eating club* sounded exclusive.

Still, she thought, no matter how stunning a meal was, it always disappeared at the end of the night. Gemstones, on the other hand, were forever.

Joaquim stood alongside her. "Would you like to do the honors?"

"You can."

He knocked on the door of the eating club. A moment later, it swung open to reveal a heavy man in a stained white apron. He was stirring a bowl of white sauce that he'd tucked under his arm.

"Yes?"

"We're here for dinner," said Joaquim.

The chef looked Ainsley up and down. "We don't accept women."

Ainsley shook her head in surprise. "Yes, you do. My friend ate here, and she's a woman."

"Tonight it's only men."

"Since when?"

He sneered at her. "Since just now."

Ainsley cocked her hip out and punched her fist into the side of her waist. That was a sign that her dignity had been injured. "This is personal, isn't it?"

"No."

"You don't want me here."

"Because you look like a problem."

She rubbed her ears. "*Excuse* me?"

"You look like a woman who would blab about *Gizon Handi* to everybody. Then word would spread. We would be overwhelmed with tourists from America. They would complain about the food. They would ask why there are no menus. They would demand low-fat entrees."

"But—"

The Basque chef wasn't done imagining the future. "Then all the regular men would be disgusted and leave this eating club. Then *Gizon Handi* is finished."

"It is amazing," said Ainsley, "that you can see all of that just by looking at me."

The chef dipped a pinky finger into his sauce and tasted it. His eyebrows lifted and a small hum of approval escaped his throat. "Yes, I am a man of many talents. That is why, for you, there is nothing tonight."

Ainsley peered around him. She could see people assembling at long tables. Plates of gorgeous purple asparagus, glops of white aioli, glasses of white wine. The smell of garlic and oil and tender vegetables reached her nostrils.

"You are obnoxious," she said.

"No, I'm a realist," he said. "Now go eat dinner somewhere else and then go for a walk." The chef looked at Joaquim, who'd remained diplomatically silent.

"You can come in."

Ainsley caught him by the sleeve. "Don't you dare."

"If she can't come in," he said, "I won't either."

"Bullshit," roared the Basque chef. His meaty hand curled around Joaquim's neck and literally pulled him into the door. Ainsley lunged after him, but the chef stood between them.

"The men are eating tonight," he said. "You can wait in the back alley and fight the feral cats for scraps at midnight."

Behind the Basque chef, Joaquim looked horribly embarrassed. "Ainsley—"

She felt the indignation rising like a tempest within her. "No, it's fine, Joaquim. I'm not angry with you. Go enjoy yourself. I'll see you back at the hotel later."

She stalked off down the street, hoping that Joaquim enjoyed his first and only meal at *Gizon Handi*, because after the savaging she was about to give the Basque chef on social media, they weren't going to have a single customer left.

CHAPTER SIX

Two hours later, with a belly full of *pinxtos* washed down by three glasses of red wine, Ainsley found herself walking through the streets of San Sebastián in a disassociated state. It felt as though she were on the outside of her body, looking in.

The basilica suddenly loomed large in front of her. That was surprising. She hadn't remembered choosing to walk here.

She watched herself trek up the steps and yank on the front doors. They were closed and locked. Then Ainsley watched herself move around to the side of the basilica. A side door, undecorated and carved quietly beneath an overhang, stood ajar. She slipped inside.

The overhead chandeliers were all lit, and a cleaning crew was roaming the floor, some using mops in the pews, others moving large buffers to polish the floor to a gleam.

Ainsley skirted the apse and found her way towards the confessional. She didn't know what to expect there. Padre Contrera himself? His daily schedule? A crystal tiara awaiting her on a pillow?

She arrived at the wooden box. A cleaning woman had opened the penitent's side and was busy using a long hand-held motor head to clean the plush kneeler.

"Excuse me," said Ainsley.

The woman shut off the motor and turned around. "What is it?"

"Did you happen to see Padre Contrera here?"

"No."

"I was supposed to meet him here."

The woman shrugged, and Ainsley felt herself crumple a little. The woman turned on the vacuum cleaner and lifted the kneeler to clean beneath it. Ainsley saw her lean further into the confessional box and pick up something from the floor.

It was an envelope. "What is your name?"

"Ainsley Walker."

The cleaning lady handed her the envelope. "He didn't forget you."

Ainsley looked down. On the front of the envelope were the words

Señorita Walker
Amante de piedras preciosas

Padre Contrera. This was definitely his handiwork.

"Thank you," said Ainsley.

"You're lucky," replied the cleaning woman. She petted the vacuum cleaner. "I almost sucked it into this little monster."

Ainsley smiled at her, then walked across the floor to a pew and sat down to open the envelope. Her hands were shaking with excitement.

Inside was a single slip of paper. On it were six lines of typewritten poetry.

Over the green hill
At the top of the cliff
That shines pink in the dark
Inside the wedding veil
That hangs woven with tears
Lies the treasure of the princess.

Ainsley stared at the paper. This was the metaphorical clue that Padre Contrera's friend had recently translated? Six lines of unrhymed poetry that sounded like they'd been written by an overwrought high school girl?

She was supposed to walk across all of northern Spain—with six lines of crappy poetry as her guide?

Ainsley folded the slip of paper and stuffed it into her purse and walked out of the basilica. A taxi pulled up just as she arrived, and when the door opened, she saw Joaquim getting out.

"Baby," he said, "I knew you'd come back here."

"That guy was an asshole."

"Absolutely," he agreed, "but an asshole who can cook the hell out of a quail."

"I'm glad you liked it."

His eyes found the document in her hand. "Tell me what you found."

"A poem. Read it."

Joaquim took the poem, and she watched his eyes going back and forth across the paper. When he was done, he handed it back. "That's pretty skimpy evidence."

"The priest said that I seemed special," she said. "He doesn't give this out to just anybody."

"But you told him that you were a gemstone investigator."

"Of course. That's why he gave it to me." She looked at him with fear in her eyes. "What do you think I should do?"

He shrugged. "Is there any way to target the part where the tiara is located?"

"It could be anywhere," she said.

"Padre Contrera said that she flung herself off a cliff, right?"

"Yes."

"So it's probably in the Picos de Europa."

"Joaquim, walk it with me," she said. "You know how to do stuff like this."

"I don't have time, little spoon," he said. "I really have to go home and work."

"Please."

He sighed and leaned against a lamppost. "You are totally out of your mind."

"Yep."

"I can't. Truly." Then he thought about it. "There's a lot of things you'll have to do."

"I know."

"You'll have to cancel your plane ticket."

"No problem."

"You'll have to buy equipment."

"Absolutely."

He paused dramatically. "You'll have to get dirty."

"For a priceless crystal tiara, I'll sleep in a pigsty." She grabbed his sleeve. "This could make me *famous*."

Joaquim looked at her with wry detachment. "This is a seriously stupid idea. I mean, this is the kind of dumb thing that teenage boys do."

"So what?"

He grinned, and their eyes locked. Ainsley leaned in and gave her boyfriend an enormous kiss. His lips felt soft.

When they pulled apart, her eyes were moist. "No crying yet," Joaquim said. "That's for the goodbye tomorrow."

CHAPTER SEVEN

In the shoe section of a local outfitter's shop, Ainsley Walker twirled the hiking boot around in her hand, searching for flaws.

Three o'clock in the afternoon, and Joaquim was already in the air. Now she was alone, preparing for a long hike with very little idea of how to do so. She did know, however, that proper shoes were needed. Her eye roved across the boots, looking for irregularities in the lacing, the top piece, the toebox.

Nearby, a salesgirl stood watching her inspect the item. "Can I help you with anything?"

"I'm looking for the perfect hiking boot."

"That one in your hand is good. It's rated for five hundred kilometers."

"Only five hundred?"

The salesgirl looked amused at Ainsley. "You are hiking the Camino?"

"Yes."

A knowing look grew on her face. "You should buy two pairs."

"Are you serious?"

"It's six hundred kilometers. Some people even need three."

Ainsley peered more closely at the object. There. Along the shank, at the edge of a stud, curled a tiny shred of leather. It was a mere speck, the size of a fly's wing, but it was a sign of shoddy production.

"I found a mistake," she said. "Right there."

The salesgirl shrugged. "There is a different pair—"

"Listen," said Ainsley, "if you give me a discount, I'll still buy."

The salesgirl weighed the negotiation. "Buy two pairs, and I'll cut thirty percent off."

"Deal."

From behind Ainsley, a man's voice cut in. "Did I hear you're walking the Camino, miss?"

The accent was a heavy Scottish brogue, but the words were English. Ainsley turned. A skinny man in a pair of light-weight hiker's khakis and a bright red windbreaker was in a nearby seat. He was trying on a new pair of walking shoes. A scraggly red beard clung pathetically to his chin.

"Yes," she said.

"Don't buy boots. This time of year, you don't need them. Just get regular shoes."

"Thank you," said Ainsley.

"Also, don't buy two pairs. The extra weight will slow you down."

"They're not heavy."

"Trust me," he said, "every gram of weight in your pack counts."

"My pack?"

He stared at her. "You do have a pack, right?"

Ainsley shook her head.

"What are you going to carry with you?"

"My suitcase." Then she added proudly: "It's on rollers."

Sighing, he stood up and stuck out his hand. "My name's Graeme. It looks like Graham but served with an extra side of Scot."

"Ainsley," she replied, shaking it.

"Miss Ainsley, I've hiked all over the world, and I'm an expert at picking out which newbies are going to get devoured by unfamiliar terrain. You're one of them."

"I'm tougher than I seem," she replied. Ainsley wasn't ready to let on that she was feeling overwhelmed.

"We Scots are experts on walking in bad weather. I insist on helping you prepare."

"Sure," said Ainsley. There wasn't any reason to turn down help.

"Follow me and take notes."

Ainsley handed the hiking boots back to the salesgirl, who made a face. Then she followed Graeme through the store.

"There are a lot of things to carry," he said, "such as earplugs. That's for the *albergues*." He tossed a package into her basket. "You wear hosiery?"

Ainsley raised an eyebrow. "No."

"Don't look at me like that. I'm wearing them right now. They prevent blisters. What about a tent?"

"What about it?"

"You need one."

"No I won't. I'll just stay in hotels."

He ground the palm of a hand into his eye. "You haven't done your research, have you?"

"This is a last-minute thing."

He tossed Ainsley a tent. "Buy this, you'll thank me. There's a lot more to say," he said, checking his watch, "but I've got an appointment in twenty minutes. When are you planning to start?"

"Tomorrow morning."

"Which camino?"

She shrugged. "I don't know. The main one, I guess."

"That's the French way."

"Okay."

Graeme regarded her warily. She noticed that, beneath the layers of hiker scruff, he had intelligent eyes.

"Miss Ainsley," he said, "I'd recommend that we start together, if our paces match one another." He hastily added: "And if your company isn't too wretched. I'm picky about my conversation."

She couldn't help but smile. "Why do you want to walk with me?"

"Honestly?"

"Yes."

"I couldn't stand feeling the guilt if I'd stumbled over your corpse being eaten by the griffin vultures."

She looked at his dirty skin, clumped hair, scratchy beard. "They'd go for you first, Graeme. You're better seasoned."

"Maybe." He smiled ruefully, a wave of sadness washing darkly over him. Ainsley felt sorry that she'd made the comment.

Then he suddenly brightened up. "Okay, tomorrow, I'll meet you at the downtown coach stop at six am. We have to catch a coach to Logroño to pick up the *francesa*."

"I'll be there."

"And be sure to buy a pack. No rolling suitcase."

They shook hands, and Ainsley watched him leave the outfitter's shop. She'd always heard that Scottish people were outrageously helpful. Now she had proof.

LOGROÑO

CHAPTER EIGHT

As Ainsley went to take her very first step on the Camino, she tripped on the curb and fell onto the ground.

"What the hell—" she said.

"Aye, miss, there's no cursing on the Camino," said Graeme.

She tried to get to her knees. "I can curse whenever I want."

"Then direct your ire," he said, helping her up, "to the manufacturer of such a deadly device as a curbed sidewalk."

They'd stepped off the coach just outside the town of Logroño. In front of them had been the famous sign, the St. James scallop shell drawn sideways and in blue on a rectangular stone marker. A thin line of brown dirt stretched between green fields and disappeared into the distance.

The Camino de Santiago.

Ainsley wiped the tiny pebbles and dirt from her hands and knees. She was dressed in a pair of jeans and her white faux fur jacket. Behind her was the purple brocade suitcase that she'd brought on the airplane. On her feet were her new hiking shoes.

Graeme looked at her and shook his head. "You didn't buy a pack."

"I didn't want to give up my suitcase."

"You're going to be a world of hurt."

"No," she said, "I'm tough."

"Me too. But just wait until it starts raining."

"I'll buy an umbrella." Ainsley lifted her foot, rotated her ankle, and shook it off. "This feels better now."

The coach pulled away, and as the motor faded into the distance, the sounds of silence began to envelope the two of them.

She noticed him looking at her.

"I bought caramels," she said.

"Good for you. But you'll need a different coat."

"Never."

"I'm not kidding."

"Neither am I. This coat is my favorite."

He shrugged. "I'll be deaf to your bitching during the first rain shower." He motioned with his arm. "Ladies first?"

Smiling, Ainsley took her first step onto the path. She felt the stones through the sole of her new hiking shoes, the instability of the gravel, the springy give of the soil below. She hoped that nobody had seen fit to improve the Camino by paving it with asphalt or, even worse, concrete. As a former track-and-field star, she had been spoiled by sprinting on a cushioned cinder track throughout high school, and today, her twenty-nine-year-old knees were exquisitely attuned to surfaces. A soft dirt path was as good as it could be on a person's joints.

Ainsley and the Scot started walking through the fields, feeling the breeze at their backs. It was a sunny morning, and the fields of yellow sunflowers nodded as they passed by, the green blades of grass bowing at their passing. A pair of pigeons circled past like a welcoming committee.

"Miss Ainsley," said Graeme, "enlighten me on what brings you to the Camino for the first time."

She thought about how to answer that question. She'd known it was coming. She could provide the truth or a multitude of lies.

She opted for the truth.

"I'm walking to find a hidden treasure," she said.

"Is that so?"

"Yes, it is."

"Tell me."

"A priest told me about a crystal tiara worn by a medieval princess. She hid it somewhere along the trail before falling to her death."

He cast his best withered eye upon her. "I took you for a bit of an eccentric when I heard you speaking in the shop yesterday. Now I'd say that you're an absolute loon."

Ainsley kept a stiff upper lip. She held her head high. "You can believe whatever you want, Graeme."

"Approximately where on the trail would this treasure be hiding?"

"I don't know exactly, but somebody gave me a secret clue. Here, read it for yourself."

She showed Graeme the ancient poem that the priest had left for her. The Scot read it to himself as they walked, his lips moving silently, his furrowed brow furrowing even further.

"A Catholic priest wrote this?" he said.

"Padre Contrera. He translated it."

He shook his head. "Never trust a priest."

Ainsley stared at him. "A priest is a holy man."

"Well, I'm Presbyterian," he replied, as if that explained everything. "Anyways, if she flung herself off a cliff, there are number of places that could've happened. We'll get to the first mountains in a couple of days."

Ainsley decided to turn the tables. "Tell me why you're doing this?"

"It's my mother's wish," he replied.

"Your mother told you to hike the Camino?"

"No," he said slowly, "it's because, soon, I'm not going to be able to see her anymore." He paused. "I think you can read between the lines."

Ainsley grew quiet. There was nothing but the crunch of gravel under their shoes for a while. Just because civilization got older didn't mean that death had been erased. It seemed that the Scot was hiking the Camino out of desperation, in search of a cure.

"I'm sorry," she said.

"We all have to go someday," he said. "We never know when."

Ainsley nodded. "I lost my father at age twelve."

He made a soft sound in his throat. "That's the worst time too. Really fucks you up."

She threw a barbed look at him. "You're not supposed to swear on the Camino."

"I made that rule up to mess with you," he said. "You can curse all you fuckin' like."

CHAPTER NINE

They walked for the rest of the morning, Ainsley dragging her rolling suitcase behind her over the gravel road. They stopped to eat a couple of packaged sandwiches that Graeme had had the foresight to buy the night before.

By one o'clock pm, gray thunderclouds had begun to roll overhead, and Ainsley stopped walking to stare straight up at the sky. She closed her eyes as the first spatter of rain landed square in the middle of her forehead.

Then the sky opened up, and soon she was drenched, hair plastered against her face.

"This way," said Graeme, huddling underneath the hood of his windbreaker. He was pointing to the left. "We'll wait it out under that building."

Now they were holed up underneath the overhang of an old vineyard operation. There was just enough space to stand against the wall. Ainsley watched the water drizzle straight down in front of her face.

"This is going to pass," he said. "I can tell."

"How do you know?"

"I'm from Scotland. We're experts at watching miserable rainstorms like this."

Ainsley pressed her back flat against the stone wall. The misty rain was obscuring the vineyard, a field of bare vines supported by rows of wires.

"Where are we going to stay tonight?" she asked.

"Najera."

"Is it far?"

"No."

"Which hotel are you planning to stay?"

"At an *albergue*," said Graeme. He had lit a small cigarillo and was smoking it contentedly. Ainsley wasn't sure how he was keeping it lit.

"Is that a hotel?"

"It's more like a dormitory."

She flared her nostrils. "Graeme, I don't think I can do that."

"Why not?"

She wrapped her coat around herself more tightly. "Because I don't share bathrooms with other people."

He laughed. "And you're walking the Camino?"

She ignored the gibe. "I'm going to find a hotel instead."

"You're welcome to try."

"Oh," said Ainsley, "I definitely will."

The Scot didn't say anything else. He just stood there, smoking quietly. Then he held the *cigarillo* up in front of his face, looked at it, and flicked it away onto the grass. A thin line of smoke ran up into the wet air as the rain extinguished the cigarillo.

"I used to love those things so much," he said.

"What happened?"

He grew sad, then shrugged. "I don't know. Just lost my taste for them." His eyes slid sideways and he took in Ainsley's outfit. "You know something," he said, "there is a tradition at the end of the Camino."

"Tell me."

"You walk all the way to Finisterre, on the ocean. Then you burn your clothing. The police don't like people doing that, but we still do it."

Ainsley unconsciously wrapped her coat around her a little more tightly. "I certainly won't be doing that," she said. "In fact, I won't even be finishing the Camino."

"No?"

She shook her head. "I'm just looking for the crystal tiara."

"So that's really all you want?"

"Yes. Once I find it, I'm out of here."

Graeme regarded his fellow traveler. "There is a spiritual aspect to walking the Camino," he said. "That's why so many undertake it."

"Good for them," said Ainsley.

"It's supposed to be a time for reflection. You know, we're supposed to think about our behavior, why we do what we do. Our place in the universe. Maybe figure out what comes in the next life."

Ainsley said nothing.

"Any thoughts?"

"Nope."

The Scot blew air out of his mouth. "I thought I left all the unreflective bastards back in my country."

"I don't need to reflect upon anything," she said. "I have a job and a boyfriend, and I enjoy both of them very much. I love fashion and style and gemstones and foreign languages. That's me. I don't have to think about it."

"There's no reason to improve yourself?"

She crossed her arms. "I like me."

He shrugged and looked away. “So be it.”

Ainsley stuck a hand out beyond the eave. “It’s starting to taper off. We can walk.”

She extended the handle of her rolling suitcase. Graeme watched her walk away, smiled ruefully, then started after her.

CHAPTER TEN

"There is not a single place to stay in this town," said Ainsley, "other than this stinking hole."

She was standing in the lobby of the *albergue* in Najera. Graeme was sitting in a chair, his bare feet propped up on a toffet. A glass of juice rested comfortably in his hand. He looked washed and rested.

"That comes as a surprise? This town is the size of a flea."

"You could've told me."

"We just met," he said, "but I can tell that nobody can tell you anything." He tilted his head. "Your hair looks different."

"Yes, it's a freaking mess."

After the rain had stopped, her hair had dried in the air, and now it was a frizzy corona of agitation. It always did this in humid weather anyways, but this was ten times bigger than usual.

For the last two hours, Ainsley had roamed up and down every single street in the village. She'd found a total of one hotel. The owner had answered the door in a nightgown, barely listened to the request, then waved her off before slamming the door.

Now she'd returned to this *albergue*. It was a nicely appointed lobby, with several chairs and sofas scattered upon the hardwood floors and heavy rugs. Table lamps and a small library completed the effect.

Ainsley marched up to the front desk. The young lady behind the desk was reading the Bible.

"Do you have a private room?" she said.

"No."

"Do you know where I can find one?"

The woman smiled. "You can sleep on the grass next to the river."

Ainsley groaned. "How many people sleep in each room?"

"Twenty."

Her nose twitched in disgust. "Can I get a single?"

The clerk shook her head. "They're all bunks."

Ainsley dropped her chin. She'd assumed that this was how pilgrims used to travel, centuries ago, not how they did it today. Still, there was nowhere else to go.

Her next words fell like tiny, cold marbles from her lips. "Then I would like ... whatever you can give me ... for the evening."

The woman looked genuinely sad. "I'm sorry, but we're already full."

Ainsley's stomach began doing backflips. "Excuse me?"

"The women's quarters are already filled up."

"Are you kidding?"

"No."

Ainsley sensed a movement behind her. A hand landed on the counter. It belonged to Graeme.

"Be a dear," he said to the clerk, "and check the reservation under my name. Graeme McRae."

The clerk looked in her reservations book. "It shows two. A man and a woman."

"This is the woman," he said.

"Very well then," said the clerk. "It looks like you do have a place to sleep tonight, Miss..."

"Walker," said Ainsley. She turned to Graeme. "You are *such* a dear."

He nodded. "Let's see how you handle the next challenge."

The clerk said, "*Credencial*, please."

Ainsley stammered, not understanding. The clerk mimed stamping a piece of paper. "Your *credencial*. I need to stamp it."

"It's a paper?"

"Yes. Your *credencial*. You don't have one?"

"No."

"How long have you been walking?"

"This is my first day."

"Oh."

The woman made a big deal of closing the Bible, then reaching beneath her desk and producing a small booklet. It looked much like a passport, except it was folded eight times, accordion style. She wrote Ainsley's name on the front, then stamped it and slid it across the counter. "You have to stamp this every time you stay at an *albergue*."

"Why?"

"So that you can collect your *compostela* at the end of the Camino."

"Thank you," said Ainsley, "but I'm not going to the end."

The clerk shrugged. "Suit yourself. You should still collect the stamps, however, just in case." She nodded with her head towards a bin. "The towels are over there, and your dormitory is the door on the left."

"What time is checkout?"

"There is no checkout," said the woman. "You wake up with everyone else at dawn and leave."

CHAPTER ELEVEN

That night, Ainsley lay in her bunk, watching the bulge in the mattress of the person sleeping above her.

All around her were the snores of the other *peregrinos*. She'd learned that word from Graeme tonight, as they'd shared a glass of wine before sleep. It was what the pilgrims on the Camino were called.

Ainsley couldn't sleep. One reason was the fact that she'd worn her clothing to bed. Another reason was the grime that she'd noticed ringing the bowl of the toilet and in the tiles of the communal showers. It was hard to get those images out from her mind.

But the biggest reason was the doubts—that she could find the crystal tiara, that it would prove to be authentic, that she could actually walk this Camino.

She plugged her ears with her fingers, trying to block out the sounds. Then she remembered that she'd purchased earplugs, on Graeme's recommendation. His advice had been a godsend so far.

Ainsley leaned over in her bunk and reached into her roller suitcase, which lay on the floor. A small black creature suddenly leapt out of the suitcase and scampered across the floor.

It was a rat.

Ainsley screamed, thrashed in her bed, and yanked her blanket up around her mouth.

The other *peregrinos* began to waken. Someone turned on a flashlight. Another muttered for her to shut up.

The woman above her hung her face over the edge of the bed. Her hair hung down in a halo around her face.

"What's the problem?" she said. She had a Dutch accent.

"There was a rat."

"Yes, they're everywhere."

"But it was in my suitcase."

"Obviously it wanted something. You weren't carrying any food in there, were you?"

Ainsley thought of the caramels in her bag.

"No," she lied.

"Then it's a mystery. Let's try to get some sleep."

The face disappeared. Slowly the sounds of other women's snoring grew in volume. It was an orchestra of snorts and snuffles.

Too terrified to reach into her suitcase for the earplugs, Ainsley lay there until dawn, eyes wide open, listening to the awful cacophony.

CHAPTER TWELVE

The next morning, Ainsley trudged down the Camino, dragging the purple rolling suitcase behind her.

Graeme walked alongside her. On his head was an unusual black cap that flopped sideways down over his ears. It had no brim, and from the center of the hat, directly over his face, hung a large scallop shell.

"What the hell are you wearing?" said Ainsley.

"A traditional *peregrino* hat," he replied.

"It looks ridiculous."

"I know, but it fits this walk. It makes me feel like I'm living history."

"No doubt."

He adjusted the hat with a touch of pride. "In the old days, this scallop shell would've protected me from thieves, allowed me to sleep in churches, and helped me beg for free meals."

"It'll definitely protect you from attractive women," said Ainsley.

"Truth be told," he said, "I've never had a problem keeping those away."

As the morning wore on, Graeme began to tell Ainsley more about the history of the Camino. It'd been walked by *peregrinos* for more than a thousand years, ever since a ninth-century hermit named Pelagius claimed that a vision of stars had led him to a field in Galicia, in northwestern Spain. In that field, he claimed to have found a tomb containing the bones of St. James, one of the twelve original apostles, lost for more than nine centuries. Add some stories of local miracles that were shrewdly spread by an early form of grassroots marketing, and the legend began to grow. In fact, the name of the final stop on the Camino, Santiago de Compostela, reflects this story. The word *Santiago* derives from *San Tiago* (Saint James), and *Compostela* is a portmanteau of *campo de la stella* (field of stars).

In the medieval era, the Camino began to boom in popularity, especially when the Catholic Church stepped in with its official backing, which it did to support the resistance of the northern Iberian peninsula to the Moorish invaders. Bridges were built to ease the pilgrims' way, hospitals were built to cure them, indulgences were sold to scam them. In 1140, a pope even commissioned the world's first travel guide, the *Codex Calixtinus*, to help pilgrims find their way along the Camino.

Then things changed.

The Black Death arrived, discouraging travel. Then a series of wars on the peninsula deterred it even more. After that, the Protestant Reformation reduced the Catholic stranglehold over European life, which led to fewer pilgrims. Still later, the rise of science, the era of reason, and ultimately the great wars of the twentieth century all contributed to the slow decline of the Camino, and the walk almost fell totally out of favor. By the nineteen eighties, only a handful of *peregrinos* still arrived in Santiago de Compostela each day.

Then things changed again—for the better.

In the last thirty years, the numbers have skyrocketed, back up to nearly two hundred thousand pilgrims a year. Fifty percent are from Spain, fifteen percent use bicycles, and more men than women finish the walk. Furthermore, to earn the *compostela*, a pilgrim now only needs to complete the final hundred kilometers of the Camino, a new rule designed to encourage people to attempt it.

As he spoke, Ainsley thought about all of the *peregrinos* who'd walked this trail, blissfully ignorant of the fact that somewhere along this path lay a hidden crystal tiara—and yet only she had a clue as to its location. A small part of her reveled in such exclusive knowledge.

Graeme suddenly stopped his lecture. "What was that poem again?"

"Which part?"

"The first two lines."

Ainsley didn't need to consult the paper. She'd memorized it. "*Over the green hill.*"

"That's what I thought," he said. "Look up there."

Ainsley lifted her head. The trail, which had been running across the rolling fields of the Rioja region, collided directly with a grass-covered mound that rose abruptly from the land like Poseidon out of the waves.

"That's the green hill," she said. "It has to be. I mean, look at it."

"Which means the pink cliff must be on the other side," Graeme said.

"We're going to find out."

Ainsley doubled her pace. Soon they were hiking up a series of short switchbacks, the blades of wild grass tickling her ankles. She switched arms, but both biceps were beginning to tire of dragging the purple suitcase behind her.

She held her breath as she approached the crest of the

hill. It felt pleasant atop this mound, the breeze caressing her skin, the sweet scent of chlorophyll in her nostrils.

At the top, Ainsley stopped dead in her tracks. She let go of her suitcase, which fell over into the mud. Alongside her came Graeme. He held a hand over his eyes and squinted at the landscape.

Before them stretched a massive plain. It was perfectly flat, all the way to the horizon. Yellow fields, dotted here and there by a stray bush, an occasional tree.

"I don't see a pink cliff," he said. "Do you see one?"

"No. What is this?"

"The meseta."

Ainsley's shoulders slumped forward. "I don't want to cross this."

"Nobody does. It's the most unenjoyable part of the Camino." He took her by the elbow. "But you're on a mission, aren't you?"

"Yes," she muttered.

"Could you live with yourself if someone else found the crystal tiara just because you got a little tired?"

"No."

"Good. This is going to take five days to cross. Six if you complain and slow us down."

"I won't."

"Then let's be off."

Straightening her shoulders, Ainsley picked up the handle of her suitcase and began to trek down the other side of the hill.

To the meseta.

CHAPTER THIRTEEN

Three days later, at seven o'clock in the morning, Ainsley knew that something was wrong when Graeme stopped eating his oatmeal.

They were arranged around the long table at that night's *albergue*. It was a small dormitory, and there had been only eight *peregrinos* overnight. The previous day had seen a grueling five-hour walk in the sun, over twenty kilometers by Ainsley's reckoning, and they'd found that places to bed for the night were few and far between. Graeme had explained the meager attendance by noting that few people had the courage to walk the meseta.

"How do you know that?" she'd said.

"I have the statistics."

He'd taken out his phone and shown her. It was called the Camino app. Ainsley had smiled at that one. There was truly an app for everything.

Now, at breakfast, she'd watched the Scot put down his spoon and stare vacant-eyed, at the opposite wall. His skin appeared sallow.

The other *peregrinos* hadn't noticed. Sitting next to

Ainsley were two French women, whom Ainsley had remembered from the trail yesterday, owing to their bright orange and yellow backpacks. They were happily hosting a lively debate about whether hiking shoes were superior to running shoes. There were also a Spanish couple, a Dutchman, one Polish person, and a Korean who wasn't talking. Ainsley had learned that the walking the Camino had become incredibly popular in that country, thanks to efforts of Catholic missionaries.

During a lull in conversation, Ainsley cleared her throat. "I have a question."

The table quieted down.

"Has anyone heard of the pink cliff?"

The Dutchman lifted a finger and nodded. "I have."

"You've seen it?"

"Indeed, personally."

"Where is it?"

"You're very close," he said, "about five hours away. I was lost and wandered off the trail."

"Is that the only way to find it?"

"Probably. Why?"

"I'm on a mission."

"What type of mission?" said the Dutchman. "Are you going to throw yourself off?"

One of the Frenchwoman threw down her napkin. "Oh, you are a beast. Typical Dutch."

"She would never do that," said the other. "This poor man needs her."

"Actually," said Ainsley, "we're not together."

The Scot managed to lift his head. "Aye, that's the truth."

"But you were walking together," said the Dutchman.

"No, she walks alone," said Graeme. "Ainsley is a ... person who ..."

His sentence trailed off, and his mouth began to feebly work itself open.

"This looks serious," said one of the Frenchwomen.

"He's going to pass out," said the other.

"No," he replied, "I'm fine—"

The spoon clattered from his hand, and his head lolled around. Several hands reached out to catch him. From the other side of the table, Ainsley watched them steady the Scot, pull out his chair, escort him across the room, and lay him down on a sofa.

Her lips tightened. They didn't really need her help. Too many cooks, spoiled broth, all of that.

That was the end of breakfast, and soon Ainsley was the only one left remaining at the table. She sat there, hands in lap, trying to figure out her feelings as the tiny bits of oatmeal hardened into scabs on the wooden bowls.

Then she heard a French voice addressing her. "Do you have *any* idea what's wrong with your friend?"

She turned her head. It was the Frenchwoman.

"No," said Ainsley.

"He looks really sick."

"Then someone needs to take care of him."

"It should be you. You were walking with him."

She shrugged. "We just met five days ago. He's not my responsibility."

"I know where you want to go," said the woman, her eyes narrowing. "The pink cliff. That was the only time you said anything. Tell me what's so special about it."

Ainsley swallowed the last of her coffee and stood up. She didn't want to answer this woman, didn't need to engage her in such accusatory talk. Instead, she went over to the sink and washed out the cup and placed it in the rack.

"That is my business," said Ainsley, "and nobody else's."

The *albergue* manager came along, a thin man with a

perpetual air of distraction. He began gathering the bowls on the table. Ainsley looked at him, then nodded towards the Scot. "I hope you can help him get better."

"The Camino has a long history of dying pilgrims," said the manager.

Jesus Christ, she thought. Quickly she tried to smooth over the comment. "I'm sure he's not dying. He probably just needs some ibuprofen."

With his arm holding the stack of bowls, the manager looked her up and down, her white coat, her purple rolling suitcase. "You're walking like *that*?"

"Of course."

"You have extra water?"

"I won't need it," said Ainsley, "but thank you for your concern."

"*Buen camino*," he said.

As she slung her pack over her shoulder, she caught sight of Graeme. One of his eyes was open and looking at her. There was an empty, helpless look in the eye.

Ainsley felt a twinge of guilt in her stomach for leaving him, but she wasn't a nursemaid. Then she pushed out of the *albergue*, wheeling the roller suitcase, and let the door slam shut behind her.

CHAPTER FOURTEEN

Midday heat.

As Ainsley lifted the water bottle to her lips, she felt the last drops of water trickle onto her tongue. She saw yellow waves vibrate across her field of vision.

Nobody had adequately warned her that this part of the walk would be so hot, so flat, so devoid of water. Maybe that's what the *albergue* owner had been trying to say. Maybe she should've listened to him. But that had been three hours and at least ten kilometers ago.

She turned around. She was in a plain covered with a low brown scrub. There had been sunflowers earlier, their yellow-and-brown faces following the orb overhead, but they were gone. The trail had trudged to a higher elevation, the vegetation had withered, and now Ainsley felt as though she had been transported into a two-dimensional landscape dreamed up by a team of science fiction landscape designers. Ainsley remembered a *peregrino* in the dormitory saying that the eerie landscapes of Spain had been the setting for many of the famous Sergio Leone spaghetti western movies.

She peered hard through her sunglasses. Straight ahead, the trail was a thin line drawn by a mysterious deity in the dirt. In the distance, a band of mountains hovered on the horizon in the heat and the haze.

That was it. Her fingers formed themselves into a fist. The pink cliff had to be there. It *had* to be.

But those mountains were at least a day away.

Upset, she wheeled her bag around through the air and smashed it onto the ground. Then she kicked it.

The kick went too far, and she felt her foot slide on a loose pebble, her hamstring hyperextend. Then it stopped, and Ainsley found herself caught in a leg-split. This was ludicrous. Arms stretched out, she strained with the effort of trying to scissor her legs back together, but they'd gone too far. She'd have to pitch over sideways on the trail to get out of this.

Then she felt hands under her elbows.

"My child," said a voice, "lift yourself."

"I can't. My legs are too weak."

"You can do it."

Drawing a deep breath, Ainsley managed to tense her abdomen, her glutes, her thighs. Her hyperextended front leg pulled back just enough to give her an extra centimeter of leverage. She was able to heel-toe her feet back together again.

Upright once more, she turned around to look at her mysterious helper. She sucked in her breath. It was a mendicant in a brown robe with a rope belt cinched around his waist, his hands folded around a Bible. She hadn't even heard him approach.

"Who are you?" she said.

"Nobody."

"Where did you come from?"

"Nowhere. I represent nothing."

"But you helped me."

He nodded. "That's what we do on the Camino. We help each other."

The mendicant reached into his sack and pulled out a bottle of water. He held it out to Ainsley. "I saw you drink the last of your own."

Ainsley hesitated. What was the purpose of this man's generosity? What was he seeking for himself? Did he roam the wild highlands of northern Spain, posing as a holy man, only to bind, gag, rape, and torture unsuspecting *peregrinos*?

As soon as these thoughts crossed her mind, Ainsley felt ashamed of herself. How poisoned had her soul become? How suspicious had modern culture made her? Out here, on the meseta, far removed from the anonymity of a large city, people actually *helped* one another, with no expectation of anything in return. She'd occasionally experienced this same generosity back home, in rural areas where passing strangers smiled at each other and neighbors asked about each other's grown children and people lost track of their own front door keys because why even bother.

"Thank you," she said.

He closed his own bag, then turned and began walking again. Ainsley felt a sudden irrational fear that this religious man was abandoning her to grapple with the harsh world.

"Wait," she said.

The mendicant stopped and turned back. His eyes were inscrutable. "You can't follow me."

"I just need help finding the pink cliff. Maybe you've seen it."

He paused. "You will find it."

"How?"

"When you're ready, it will present itself."

The man in the brown robe smiled, then turned and walked away. Ainsley began to say something else, but the words caught in her throat. She watched the man disappear into the shimmering heat waves.

Then she began to walk too.

Towards the peaks.

CHAPTER FIFTEEN

As she drew closer to the mountain range, one step after another, Ainsley noticed a burning sensation on her wrist.

She looked down. It was the orange plastic wrist strap, the trendy one indicating self-empowerment, the one that Joaquim had needled her about. Underneath the plastic, her wrist had grown hot and sweaty, and small strip of red bumps had risen on her skin. It looked like a heat rash.

Ainsley tried to remember why she'd bought the thing to begin with. Had she grown that susceptible to a trend? Over the years, she'd watched many fashions drift in and out—mall hair, plaid flannel, ugg boots, leggings, yoga pants. She'd resisted all of them, until now. Something had changed—was it her? Had she become one of the trendoids?

Ainsley thought about it.

In this way, yes, she had.

It was a stunning admission. It was so strong that Ainsley stopped walking. There was only one way out of it.

She dug her fingers beneath the plastic strap, tugged it off her hand, and threw the bracelet as far as she could into the field. It disappeared into a patch of high weeds. Then she picked up the handle of her rolling suitcase and continued walking.

It'd been a shackle on her wrist, and now that she was free of it, Ainsley somehow felt a little more like herself.

Two hours later, it was late afternoon, and the mountains were looming larger, but to Ainsley's dismay she saw that the trail was heading away from the range. How many heights were there from which a princess could've flung a tiara?

Then something caught her eye.

Something pink.

She wasn't imagining it. There'd been a flash of pink in the mountains. Ainsley stopped walking, took a step backwards, tilted her head. She'd been looking at these mountains all day and hadn't seen that until just now.

It flashed again.

She looked more closely. It was coming from a short but sheer cliff nestled into the side of one of the mountains.

Ainsley turned and looked at the setting sun. It was about thirty degrees from the horizon. She had two hours left, maybe more, of daylight.

She turned back. Another flash of pink. She remembered the rhyme.

At the top of the cliff
That shines pink in the dark

Like a clap of thunder, she suddenly understood. *Shining pink in the dark* simply meant sunset, as darkness was approaching. In fact, the evening blackness had already begun to creep up from behind the mountains.

Another flash of pink, but this time the glow stayed longer. As the minutes ticked by, she watched the cliff begin to change. It was glowing pink.

Ainsley chewed on her lip as she consulted her map. By her estimate, she was about two hours from the next *albergue*, but she couldn't be sure of that. Graeme would've known for sure, or maybe his app, but neither of them were here right now. She felt a touch of guilt for abandoning the Scot, but he'd known how seriously she wanted the crystal tiara. A priceless piece of jewelry was the only object that could get her out on this blasted piece of remote land.

She weighed the options. If she attempted to make it there by nightfall, she might make it. Or she might not. Ainsley imagined her embarrassment at having to sleep by the side of a river and waking up in the morning only to find out the *albergue* was on the opposite bank.

No matter what, she'd have to backtrack two more hours tomorrow. That would mean four extra hours of walking, maybe more.

The other option was equally bad. She could spend the night here, on the meseta, and attack the pink cliff at first light.

It would mean sleeping in the tent.

Ainsley moodily kicked a pebble. This was Sophie's choice. Both options were equally lousy.

The sun had sunken lower, the sky streaked with orange and red fingers. She looked at the path winding ahead of her, imagined the hundreds of kilometers remaining. Then she looked towards the mountains, smelled the dry, baked brush, listened to the cry of an eagle overhead.

She made her decision.

Drawing a deep breath, Ainsley stepped off the Camino and began dragging her suitcase across the baked fields towards the pink cliff.

CHAPTER SIXTEEN

Two hours later, with the sun dangling perilously low on the horizon, Ainsley finished setting up her tent at the base of the mountain.

She was cutting it close. She hadn't been able to resist spending a few precious minutes of twilight preparing for the morning excursion. A few steps away, she'd followed a switchback trail that zigzagged its way up the mountain through jagged pieces of granite shelves. She'd marveled at the slabs that thrust themselves out of the earth at odd diagonals, like the sterns of ships sinking beneath the waves.

The trail had hit a dead end at the base of the pink cliff. She'd spread her hands on the granite and pressed her face against it, feeling its heat against her cheek. Then she'd pulled back and analyzed the rock closely. There were tiny veins of pink quartz running through.

She'd looked up at the bluff towering overhead. Fifty meters high, true, but it wasn't nearly as sheer as it had seemed from the trail. In fact, she'd been able to spot some iron handgrips bolted into the rock, as well as a smattering of primitive steps cut into the side.

In other words, somebody used this path regularly. Otherwise, there was no reason to go through the difficulty of bolting and chiseling. The question, of course, was who had done so—and if that person had known anything about the existence of a crystal tiara in the mountains above.

Then Ainsley had retraced her steps down the path and chosen the site for her tent. She'd picked a place not on the plain itself, but slightly elevated, in case of floods or fires. Setting up the tent had been surprisingly easy. There were four legs in collapsible segments, four sleeves, and four pegs. She slid the legs into the sleeves and stepped on the pegs, driving them into the ground. The legs bowed out, the nylon fabric flew out, and Ainsley was suddenly looking at her very own tent.

Now, the air growing chillier, she donned her coat and rummaged around inside her suitcase for her emergency meal. Graeme had given her a couple of MREs, which was U.S. military parlance for *meal-ready-to-eat*. She found them and looked at the labels. One was pasta primavera; the other, beef stroganoff.

She chose the pasta, propped up the cardboard slat, snapped the burner pack, and sat down on a rock to watch the chemical reaction occurring inside the packet. Within a minute, she could hear the sizzling. A minute after that, she ripped open the hot plastic package with quick movements of her fingertips. She used the little plastic fork and knife to wolf the food into her mouth. It scalded her tongue, but she was hungry enough that she didn't care.

Then Ainsley watched the sun lower and crash behind the edge of the earth. As blackness blanketed her campsite, she'd retreated into her tent and stretched out on the hard ground. It was awful. She unzipped her suitcase and used her extra clothing to make a sleeping pad and then laid down again.

It was still awful.

She pulled out her flashlight and began to read, a short history of the Camino that she'd filched from the *albergue*. Ainsley usually loved reading, and she tried to immerse herself in the history of St. James, his death in Iberia, the centuries that had elapsed between his death and the discovery of his remains that were being kept in a golden vessel in the cathedral in Santiago de Compostela.

She set down the book. She just couldn't get into the story. She found it hard to believe that hundreds of thousands of people had bought into this silly legend of the field of stars and God's will to vanquish the Moors.

A few hours later, her body turned sideways on the floor of the tent, her hands cupped under her left cheek, Ainsley had fallen into a light sleep.

That's when the first howl sounded across the plain.

CHAPTER SEVENTEEN

Ainsley's eyes flew open.

She held still, her leg muscles tense, as the eerie sound echoed like a high warning across the fields. The animal was clearly far away, but that wasn't much comfort. She knew how animals could move, and there were few living things here on the meseta.

Then silence returned to the landscape. She listened to the wind whistling, the thin nylon walls of the tent flapping. She flipped over to her right side, closed her eyes, and tried to doze off again.

A couple of hours later, the howl sounded again. Ainsley's eyes flew open again. That one sounded much closer. She crawled to the door of the tent and peered outside.

The moon had risen overhead, and its light beamed across the land. The effect was strong enough to take Ainsley's breath away. The landscape looked ghostly and lunar, bleached white against the darkness of the night sky.

And then she saw a movement.

Far off, maybe a kilometer, a dark creature was slinking through the brush—and it was coming her way. Another movement caught her eye. It was a second creature. She spotted a third, then a fourth.

It was a pack of dogs.

Wild dogs.

Graeme had mentioned that they lived out here, that they sometimes harassed and even attacked *peregrinos*. Ainsley cursed her own stupidity. She should never have prepared hot food out here. The scent was probably attracting a galaxy of wild animals from all over the meseta.

She glanced again at the small shapes on the plain. They were moving quickly, and she could see them crossing and recrossing each other. They would arrive very soon, and she suspected that this wasn't a pack of golden retrievers. There was no telling what wild dogs would do.

Ainsley wasn't going to wait around to find out, either. She chewed on a fingernail while she racked her brain. There was only one place to go where the dogs wouldn't be able to follow her.

The pink cliff.

She hurriedly threw all of her clothing back into her rolling suitcase. Then Ainsley zipped it shut and pulled it outside and quickly began to disassemble the tent. Soon she grew frustrated. The collapsible segments of the legs were getting pinched in the sleeves. To dismantle them was going to require both time and fine motor coordination.

The yipping sounded again, this time at a higher pitch. Ainsley knew that meant the dogs were growing closer.

She gave up on the tent. Forcing herself to stay calm, she put on her coat, grabbed her rolling suitcase, and began to quickly move up the switchbacked trail. The wheels of her suitcase bounced and rutted across the uneven granite surface. The edges of the fabric, scraping the granite on every hairpin turn, were soon shredded.

At last she reached the top of the trail. The sun was

starting to rise behind the mountain. She looked up. The cliff was a black monolith silhouetted against a faintly orange sky.

The howls sounded from below her. Then she heard the scraping of metal on rock.

The tent.

They were destroying the thing. She remembered why. She'd left the dinner packets inside. The leftover plastic sleeve of pasta. The untouched beef stroganoff.

Then something dawned on Ainsley. If they were destroying a tent to get a few licks of primavera sauce, they might go through even more to corner and attack a live human being.

Ainsley looked at her battered suitcase. It was beautiful, but it hadn't been designed for this type of off-road abuse. Graeme had been right. She should've brought a backpack.

Now she would have to leave the suitcase behind.

The thought physically sickened her, but there was no time to waste. Ainsley reached inside and found her small jewelry bag and stuffed it into her left pocket of her coat. Then she tried to put her favorite pair of heels into her right pocket, but they wouldn't fit. Sighing, she placed them back in the suitcase and closed it and zipped it shut and sat the luggage on its side. She'd be back to pick it up soon.

If the dogs didn't get to it first.

Ainsley slung her purse around her opposite shoulder and tightened the strap. It was tucked into her armpit now.

She turned to face the cliff. She placed the toe of one shoe onto the first ledge dug into the side of the rock and began to pull herself up.

CHAPTER EIGHTEEN

Ainsley clung to the side of the cliff like a spider monkey.

The movements were simple. *Hand to iron grip, hold. Foot to ledge, hold. Then pull.* The ledges were deep enough, the grips secure enough, the angle of the cliff relaxed enough that she didn't feel too frightened. After all, she'd scaled the rock wall at her health club many times, and this wasn't much different.

Except for the fact that there was no safety harness.

Not daring to look down, Ainsley kept a slow but steady pace. *Hand to iron grip, hold. Foot to ledge, hold. Then pull.*

She didn't dare to stop. A personal trainer had once told her that the climber who stops moving is the climber who feels fear.

Far below, the wild dogs were howling and snarling. Ainsley wondered if they'd run up the switchbacks and broken into her luggage, if they were so savage that they'd started to fight one another.

Then the iron grips ended halfway up the cliff, and she pulled herself up to her feet. She was standing on a narrow ledge, less than a meter wide. It stretched away to the right for ten meters, after which it plunged into a small tunnel.

Ainsley began to panic, until she noticed that someone had bolted a thin rope into the side of the wall. Ainsley willed herself to calm down.

She would have to edge along sideways.

With hands on the rope and face pressed to the cliff, Ainsley began to shuffle along the ledge, her feet splayed sideways in first position, making tiny ballerina steps. Her heel kicked a pebble, and it skittered along the cliff and fell off the ledge. She didn't hear it hit the bottom. She listened to the grating and buzzing of the insects as the fields began to stir with life. There was no sign of the dogs.

A gust of wind kicked up. She stopped moving, pressing herself against the stone wall. The wind lifted her hat off her head and carried it far away out of sight. Ainsley gritted her teeth. She'd already left enough behind.

A minute later, the wind died down, and with wobbly legs, Ainsley finished the crossing. She crouched in the mouth of the small tunnel, trying to breathe, steadying her nerves. She ran her fingertips along the rough surface of the rock walls. It had been done by hand. She tried to imagine the days, weeks, months, and years it'd taken.

On her hands and knees, Ainsley crawled through the tunnel. The sharp knobs of rock dug into the tender places on either side of her kneecaps, and the soft flesh of her palms was soon scraped.

She emerged from the tunnel, blinked in the morning light, and stood up. Ainsley found herself in a glade, surrounded on three sides by high granite walls. On the ground, a few tufts of grass sprouted from the thin layer of soil that lay on top of the rock.

In front of her was an old wooden ladder that had been bolted into the granite wall. She craned her neck and looked up. The rungs seemed to stretch on forever. She guessed that there were at least fifty.

She spun around. There was no other path out of the glade.

Ainsley drew a deep breath and then released it. Then she dropped her head. She was beginning to regret her decision to pursue the crystal tiara.

Tentatively, she placed her right foot on the first rung, her hands on the second, and began to climb.

It was slow going. While the first part of the cliff had been gently angled, this was nearly perpendicular to the ground. She felt trembling beginning in her limbs but refused to acknowledge it.

Five, ten, fifteen, twenty rungs. As she grew more exposed on the rock face, Ainsley felt the wind growing stronger, the air growing chillier.

Then the toe of her shoe slipped against a rung, her body lurched, and panic flashed through her body. Her fingers instantly seized up in a ferocious grip on the rung. Ainsley shut her eyes and pressed her forehead against the ladder. She needed to stay calm. Her other foot had remained stable, and now all four were good. There was no reason to panic.

But her body didn't care. It wasn't moving.

She tried to pry her fingers from the rung, but they refused to obey. They stayed gripping the rung for dear life. Ainsley had become a prisoner of her own fear.

Overhead, she sensed something circling. She craned her head to the sky, squinching an eye against the growing daylight. It was a circle of large, dark birds. Those must be the griffin vultures that Graeme had mentioned. He'd said that they were almost always hungry because EU regulations force farmers to burn their dead animals quickly.

She imagined that they were quick to pick off any hiker who'd fallen from a cliff.

Ainsley hung onto the ladder like that for what felt like an eternity, thinking about the situation. Her eyes were filling with tears. Then she sensed another movement above her.

She looked up. At the top of the ladder, a human was beginning to climb down the rungs.

Shit.

Ainsley thunked her head against the ladder and ground her teeth together in sheer frustration. This ladder wasn't wide enough for two. Why hadn't this guy waited for her to reach the top? Didn't anybody in Spain think *ahead*?

She waited while the figure slowly made its way down the ladder. As the person drew closer, Ainsley noticed the apple-shaped bottom, the stumpy legs, the layers of petticoats. Then she heard the person humming a melody. It was a high and flute-like voice.

It was a woman.

CHAPTER NINETEEN

The woman in the petticoats looked down at Ainsley, only three rungs below. Her face was a mask of good cheer.

"You're in trouble," she said.

"I got scared," replied Ainsley.

"It happens to everybody. Here's what you do." The woman reached into her petticoats and produced a small leather bladder. "Drink two mouthfuls of this. Only two."

"But—"

"No *but*. You have to do it. Ready? Put your hand up and catch it."

Ainsley realized that the woman was about to drop the bladder onto her head. With incredible effort, she managed to unpeel her right hand from the rung and force her palm open. The tendons in her wrist ached from the death grip.

The bladder came whistling down through the air. Ainsley caught it.

"Now drop it," said the woman.

"Why?"

"It's empty. Just drop it to the ground. I'll get it later." She grinned. "Always test first. I learned that the hard way." The woman reached into her petticoats and produced a second bladder. It looked noticeably fuller. "This is the real one."

Ainsley dropped the empty bladder and watched it float softly to the grass below. The woman dropped the second one, and Ainsley caught it. She flicked off the cap with her thumb and lifted it to her mouth and drank. Her mouth was filled with the taste of a sweet liquor.

"Cherry cordial," said the woman. "It's homemade. Please don't spit up."

Ainsley clicked the cap back on and stuffed it into her coat pocket. Already she could feel the warmth spreading through her body. Seven am, hanging on a ladder on the side of a mountain, getting drunk. Life didn't always have to make sense.

"Now, do as I do," the woman in the petticoats said. "Left foot up."

Ainsley lifted her left foot to the next rung.

"Good. Right hand up."

She lifted her right hand.

"Left hand."

Done.

"Now the hard one. Be brave, ready? Left foot—go."

Ainsley whimpered under her breath but managed to hoist up her left foot to the next rung.

"You did it," said the woman in the petticoats. "Now, repeat that eighteen more times, and you'll be at the top."

Ainsley groaned, but she knew the woman was right. Over the fifteen minutes, she concentrated on moving one limb at a time. She felt her body loosen up after that cherry cordial. Even her face and lips were looser, warmer.

Finally, Ainsley hoisted herself over the top rung of the ladder and flopped onto the rock. She lay on her back, breathing, her purse still tucked underneath her arm.

The woman in the petticoats sat on a rock. She pulled a

cracker from her petticoats and began to munch on it. Ainsley wondered how much stuff she kept in there.

"You've been walking for a long time?" she said.

"Three days."

"A short camino."

Ainsley pulled herself up to a sitting position. "I'm not walking the Camino. I'm searching for something."

The woman in the petticoats regarded Ainsley oddly. "Everybody on the Camino is searching for something."

"No," said Ainsley, "I'm looking for an object."

The woman grew interested. "Tell me."

Ainsley wasn't sure if she could trust the woman, so she avoided the question, lifted herself to her feet, and unbuttoned her coat. Her fingers were finally loosening up. "First, tell me about you. What are you doing here?"

"This is where I live."

"Up *here*?"

The woman nodded.

"It must be lonely," said Ainsley.

"Sometimes. But I get visitors." The woman nodded to the ladder. "Usually they come the same way that you did."

Then the woman in the petticoats pulled something out of her mouth. Ainsley realized it was a set of false teeth. She held them up in the air and studied them in the morning light. Then she shrugged and stuffed them back into her mouth.

Suddenly Ainsley decided she could trust this woman. Anybody comfortable enough to show a mouthful of gums to an absolute stranger probably wasn't hiding anything. Furthermore, she was a local, which meant that she had knowledge that might be helpful.

"I'm searching for a crystal tiara," said Ainsley.

The woman arranged her petticoats. "I don't know anything about that."

"Here, look at this."

She pulled Padre Contrera's poem from her bag and held it out. The woman took the paper from her hand and held it directly up to her face. She was nearsighted to the point of blindness.

As the woman's head physically moved left and right across the paper, Ainsley explained everything—the confessional, Padre Contrera, the poem, the cancelled flight, the walk thus far.

"And since this is the pink cliff," said Ainsley, "the next step is to find the wedding veil."

The woman in the petticoats tapped her index finger on her lips. "I think I know this wedding veil."

Ainsley felt her heart thump. "Can you show me?"

"First, I need to show you something."

"I don't really have time," said Ainsley.

"But I had the time to save you from yourself on the ladder. Now you can make time for me."

The woman's eyes were straining to leap out of her skull. Her expression was utterly serious.

Ainsley lowered her chin to her chest. "All right, fine."

A broad country smile came across the woman's face. She hiked up her petticoats and brushed off her boots. "Let's go. Stay close to me."

She turned and took off down a narrow trail. Ainsley hesitated for a fraction of a second before following.

CHAPTER TWENTY

For the next hour, the trail carried the two women into the far reaches of the mountain range.

A heavy fog rolled across the path, obscuring Ainsley's sight. Feeling her way around blind curves, hurrying past drop-offs, she stayed as close as possible to the sturdy little woman in the petticoats. It wasn't easy. The woman had no fear, and her short legs navigated the uneven granite surface of the trail with an expertise that only comes with years of practice.

At last they broke into a small high-altitude valley, and the sight was enough to take Ainsley's breath away.

To the left and the right were immensely steep slopes, covered in scraggly vines and brush. So great were their inclines that nothing short of a mountain goat could traverse them. The valley floor itself was narrow, maybe twenty meters across, and no more than a hundred meters deep. It was covered in a bed of deep, springy grass.

A primitive hut squatted at the back of the valley, nestled against the wall of the mountain. It was made of rocks that seemed to have been quarried from this very valley. They had been carefully stacked upon one another—no trusses, no I-joists, not even any mortar. It truly looked like a relic from the Stone Age. Ainsley half expected to see a Cro-Magnon woman emerge from the doorway with a baby hanging from her filthy teat.

As they crossed the springy grass, however, she noticed that a small arch had been carefully laid over the front door. Then she spotted a modest cross erected behind the structure.

"Is this a chapel?" said Ainsley.

The woman in the petticoats nodded. "It dates from the ninth century."

Ainsley tried to put that in perspective. When this chapel was built, most people still got their stories by saying them to each other, and English was still a guttural Germanic dialect that wouldn't be injected with any technical Latin words for two hundred more years. It would be four hundred more years until a young man named Chaucer set down the story of medieval pilgrims telling stories to one another, and another seven hundred years until a thirty-year-old actor at the Globe Theater in London began penning his own plays.

In other words, this chapel was *really* old.

"What do you do here?" asked Ainsley.

"I am the groundskeeper," she replied.

Ainsley wondered why a groundskeeper would be needed here. The site wasn't exactly accessible to tourists, and usually such remote places were left to fall into ruins.

"Now," said the woman, "you must come inside. There is something I want to show you."

Ainsley followed the woman up to the front door of the chapel. She had to duck her head to enter.

The interior was the decorative equivalent of a pig grunt. The stone floor was uneven and damp. A few rough-hewn pews sat hunched on the stones like the misshapen humps of peasant laborers. Ainsley wondered who'd dragged the wood all the way up here.

At the front of the chapel was an altar. It was little more than a few planks of pine that had been strapped together with two braces of iron, balanced across two piles of stone. And on that altar stood a single object.

A golden vessel.

It was squared off, each of the four sides made of glass, even though the top, bottom, and corners were gold. Inside the vessel was a mushy brown substance. Ainsley felt her eyes go wide, and her stomach began to churn. It was one of the weirdest things she had ever seen.

"Tell me what I'm looking at," she said.

"Seven centuries ago," began the woman, "there was a priest who lived in this valley. Because he was a priest, he had the power of transubstantiation." She noticed Ainsley's confusion. "That happens when a priest blesses a communion wafer, and it turns into the body of Christ."

That sounded doubtful, but Ainsley held her tongue. "Okay."

"That is what you're looking at today. Inside that vessel lays the body of Christ."

Ainsley felt her stomach churn. She realized that the mushy brown substance was supposedly human flesh, decaying and composting back into a weird jelly.

Then she looked more closely. Pressed against one pane of glass was a small tuft of brown fur.

It wasn't human flesh.

It was just a dead animal.

She viewed her guide with astonishment. A member of the twenty-first century, this woman had filled a jar with road-kill in order to preserve this medieval hoax, this fake relic that had been created to draw masses of *peregrinos* desperate to save their souls.

Ainsley felt sick to her stomach. She forced herself to look out the doorway, trying to imagine what this small mountain valley had looked like in the thirteenth century. She pictured a parade of filthy and exhausted pilgrims dragging themselves past rows of souvenir stands. She heard the sellers of indulgences hawking their certificates, smelled the home-brew on the drunken friars in ugly tonsures, saw the lecherous wives crooking fingers at the best-looking young pilgrims.

These people were all gone now, but this woman was keeping the old custom alive. *Fleece the tourists*. Ainsley began to wonder what other crap she kept in those petticoats. A dried apple ring passed off as the foreskin of Jesus? Stolen packets of ketchup relabeled as the blood of Christ?

Ainsley smiled politely. "That's very interesting."

"It is." The woman's eyes were dancing. "Come, let's pay our respects to it."

"No, I really can't—"

The woman took her by the elbow. "You must."

Together they approached the altar. Ainsley noticed that there was a kneeler already waiting. She also noticed the donation box next to it.

The woman hiked up her petticoats and dropped to her knees. Ainsley kneeled alongside her and kept her eyes averted from the vessel. She could almost smell the rotting tissue.

The woman in the petticoats clasped her hands and began to pray out loud. It had a heavy rhythm, every fourth syllable accented, much like an incantation. At last she finished, and the woman made the sign of the cross. Then she turned to Ainsley.

"I prayed," she said, "that you would have a *buen camino*."

"Thank you, but I'm not walking the Camino," replied Ainsley.

"Oh, this again." A shrewd look passed over her face. "What are you looking for again?"

"I have to find a wedding veil."

The woman in the petticoats nodded. "I know where it is too."

"You already said that you would help me."

The woman tapped the donation box with a finger. "First you help me. Then I help you."

Ainsley felt crestfallen. It was going to be pay-for-play. It shouldn't have surprised her. She'd greased countless skids before, but this time she'd been hoping for something a bit more elevated.

She reached into her bag, produced a five euro note, and stuffed it into the wooden box. The woman in the petticoats tapped the box again. Her eyes were pleading.

Jesus. This was almost extortion. The woman had everything but a gun in her hand. Rolling her eyes, Ainsley found a ten euro note and stuffed that into the box too.

"Is that enough?" she said.

A big smile broadened her face. "Yes, I'm very happy."

"Then show me the wedding veil."

"Of course." The woman stood up from the kneeler, groaning. "My legs ache. There must be rain coming. This way."

The woman in the petticoats stumped outside the chapel and back into the valley. She swiftly found a well-hidden trail on the far side of the left. It led between a small copse of trees. Ainsley hadn't even noticed it when she'd come in.

They walked into the copse, and then the woman stopped. Ahead was a crack in the side of the mountain. The trail snaked in between two high rock walls, merely a meter apart, and disappeared. The gray light of the misty morning died in the entrance.

"You go through there," she said, "and on the other side you will see the wedding veil."

"I don't understand," said Ainsley. "Is it an actual veil? Made of silk?"

"You will discover that on your own. Don't worry—you won't miss it."

The woman gave her weird lopsided grin, clapped Ainsley on the back, and returned up the path to the chapel.

Confused, Ainsley turned and walked into the gap.

CHAPTER TWENTY-ONE

As Ainsley plunged into the narrows, another dense wave of fog rolled through the mountains, and billowed from behind her, engulfing the trail. She couldn't see more than an arm's length in front of her. It felt like she was pushing through moist cotton.

Her arms spread out wide, she felt her way along the path, dragging her fingertips against the scraggly rock on either side. Under her feet, the mossy trail rose and fell, her feet splashing across trickles of water.

Then the narrows grew even narrower, until they were barely shoulder width apart. Ainsley could smell the wet stones, felt the millions of years of sedimentary power that had compressed them. It was a loud, crushing silence.

Then the walls squeezed even tighter, the ground grew wetter. Ainsley was forced to shuffle along sideways, leading with her shoulder. Breath steamed out of her nostrils. Under her shirt, beads of sweat began to roll down her back.

She felt something crawling along her shirt. She looked down and saw a spider. She stifled a scream, brushed it off, and kept moving.

A moment later, the fog lifted but the gulch stayed dark and wet. She looked up. There was a narrow crack of blue sky far overhead. This wedge of earth probably saw ten minutes of sunlight each day.

The walls pressed in even closer. Ainsley's chest and shoulder blades were now scraping the walls as she inched along. She sucked in her abdominals in order to squeeze past a bit of jutting rock, but it still caught on her blouse and tore a small gash in the fabric.

Ahead, Ainsley caught sight of a vertical shaft of blue sky. The narrows were coming to an end. With new energy, she charged her way through the passage, her cheeks puffing, her eyelids burning, until at last—

—she burst out into the fresh air.

She stood there, panting, feeling her shirt sticking to her skin, and looked around. She was standing in a small meadow. Despite its altitude above the dry meseta, this glade was blooming with greenery. There were high grasses, wild shrubs. A stand of oaks occupied the center of the glade.

Then Ainsley became aware of a sound. It was water thundering on rocks, forceful and endless. She looked through the trees and spotted the source of the music.

A waterfall.

That explained the lushness of this glade. Feeling the natural draw of rushing water, Ainsley hopped down the small slope, spotted a faint path through the trees, and began hiking through the small woods. The twisted arms of the oak trees dragged across her shoulders like long twiggy fingers trying to ensnare her.

Brushing them off, she emerged at the edge of a pond and stood transfixed. Before her was the waterfall, a white curtain of water at least two meters wide, and just thick enough to be opaque. It was crashing into a green pool ringed with slippery stones. Ainsley noticed that the trail continued on the other side of the pond, switchbacking up the steep cliff along the cataract, before disappearing on the ridge above.

She couldn't see how to get to the other side.

Ainsley stood there, hypnotized, for what felt like an hour. Then the revelation struck her like a thunderclap.

Inside the wedding veil
That hangs woven with tears—
Lies the treasure of the princess.

This waterfall was the wedding veil. And the falling sheets of water resembled the tears of the princess, as she'd been carted down the Camino towards an unhappy marriage. Ainsley felt the excitement building in her stomach as she realized what the final segment of the poem meant.

To find the crystal tiara, she needed to go inside the waterfall.

If it were truly that easy, though, somebody should've already discovered the treasure. The woman in the petticoats was not to be underestimated either. She might've claimed it for herself already. She'd proven herself to be a slippery character.

Then again, Padre Contrera said that he'd made the translation only recently, and as far as she knew, priests never lied, at least not without a purpose. And it wouldn't have served any purpose to lie to Ainsley.

A small movement caught her eye. She traced it to the side of the cliff, alongside the waterfall. Two small figures were moving up the switchbacks.

Ainsley squinted and studied them more closely. One was carrying a bright orange pack, and the other had a bright yellow hat.

It was the French women. The ones from the *albergue* the previous morning, the ones who'd chided her for leaving Graeme.

Ainsley felt a flurry of emotions beating in her breast. First was confusion at how those women got here. They must've passed her at some point, maybe along the Camino yesterday. Next came a wave of happiness at seeing familiar faces.

Finally came a dreadful feeling of suspicion. What on earth would those women be doing here? Nobody stumbled upon this place by accident. Nobody hiked across open fields, switchbacked through the granite shelves, climbed a massively high ladder, dealt with the woman in the petticoats, then squeezed through those narrows—all while wearing large backpacks—without a reason.

No, these women intended to come here. And Ainsley suspected that it was the same reason as her own.

She remembered one of the women insinuating that she'd known the reason for Ainsley's abandonment of Graeme.

There seemed to be only one conclusion.

The French women had known about the crystal tiara too.

Which meant that Padre Contrera *had* lied to her.

Her fists tightened themselves into balls. She should never have trusted that priest. Maybe this had all been a sick game for him. Maybe he'd given that same translated puzzle to three or four different women in his confessional last week,. women like her.

Ainsley stopped herself from going any further down that line of thinking. She'd probably just been overreacting. Just because the French women had been here didn't necessarily mean that the crystal tiara had been found. In reality, there was only one way to find out.

She had to go behind the waterfall.

CHAPTER TWENTY-TWO

Ainsley removed her hiking shoes and tied the laces together and slung them over the strap of her bag. Then she took off her socks and balled them up and stuffed them into one of the shoes.

She walked to the edge of the pond and cautiously put one foot into the green water.

It was freezing.

She yanked her foot back. That was snowmelt, without a doubt, which meant that it was too cold for wading. She looked around for a way through the waterfall.

Her eyes landed upon a trail of flat-topped rocks that led across the pond. They stopped directly in front of the deafening cascade. Most of the rocks were above water, a few slightly below the surface. All of them were undoubtedly slippery.

Ainsley put her shoes and socks back on. There was no other choice. Then she drew in a breath and steeled herself for the crossing.

Her first hop landed her square in the middle of a flat

rock. She silently thanked Graeme for his advice about shoes. These were serving her well.

She leapt to the second with no problem either. Gathering her courage, she jumped onto the third, which was level with the water, but it was much more slippery than she'd judged. Her foot slid sideways on the invisible scum, and she crashed onto her left side, soaking her left arm and left leg.

Cursing, she picked herself up and stepped to the fourth rock, which was dry. Her clothing was dripping wet and her forearm felt numb from the shock.

Then she realized that the left pocket of her coat was empty.

Her small bag of jewelry.

Ainsley swore out loud, cursing God, cursing the universe. She jumped back to the third rock, more carefully this time. Standing toe-deep in freezing water, she looked down into the icy green pond. She couldn't see the bottom.

Her bag of jewelry was down there. If she wanted to recover it, she would have to go diving in an algae-filled pond of icy snowmelt.

There wasn't much other choice. She couldn't take the risk of lowering her core temperature, not out here in the wild Spanish mountains, without a single person knowing her location. It was a fool's errand.

She would have to leave it.

She stared at the surface of the pond, thinking of all the pieces that she'd lost in there. A topaz necklace. A pair of pearl earrings. A silver bracelet.

All of them, gone.

Miserable, she began jumping across the rocks again. First her bracelet, then her suitcase, then her hat. That bag of jewelry was the fourth item that the Camino had forced her to surrender. She wondered how many more there would be, and whether the crystal tiara would be worth the sacrifice.

Several more hops, and one more slip later, Ainsley was standing before the waterfall, feeling the spray bouncing off the rocks and misting her face. It was deafening here. She glanced around for an easy way to get behind the waterfall. There wasn't one.

It was going to be straight through the water.

Shielding her bag with her hunched torso, Ainsley crouched, drew in a deep breath, and burst through the cataract like a battering ram. The sheet of freezing water pummeled her shoulders for the briefest of instants—

—and then she was on the other side.

Ainsley looked around. She was in the mouth of a well-lit cave. As the sunlight filtered through the waterfall, rainbows prisms danced happily on the walls like a thousand fairies, luring her into the darkness.

She wiped the water off her face, then tried to run a brush through her hair. It got stuck. She gave up and resigned herself to the fact that draped across her head was a tangled tornado of hideousness. At least there was nobody here to see it.

Ainsley took a few tentative steps, then a few more. The air grew chiller, and a dull ache spread onto the backs of her hands. She felt the tip of her nose growing colder. In a patch of dirt she spotted the familiar tread of another hiking shoe. That was probably the French women.

Soon the light grew fainter, and the cave dimmed, and ahead in the brown recesses of the cavern Ainsley spotted something unusual.

She picked her way towards the object, and as she drew nearer, she could make it out better.

It was an iron cage.

The size of a small bucket, the cage must have been gorgeous at one time. Now, however, its filigreed sides had been discolored with rust spots. The front door had been unlatched. She guessed that it hadn't been closed for centuries. Once priceless, today it wouldn't even fetch fifty dollars at a garage sale.

Ainsley crouched down and peered inside the cage.

It was empty.

She scrunched up her nose. There was no doubt in her mind that, once upon a time, the crystal tiara had resided here. She had deciphered the metaphors in the instructional poem correctly. Green hill, pink cliff, wedding veil—she seemed to have interpreted everything properly.

But the crystal tiara wasn't here.

This meant that somebody had beaten Ainsley to the treasure. She knew who it was too, and the thieves were getting further away with every passing second.

Ainsley stood up, turned, and ran out of the cave.

CHAPTER TWENTY-THREE

As she rounded the thirty-ninth switchback, Ainsley felt her lunch starting to rise in her esophagus.

She stopped walking. It hadn't been much of a meal, just a bag of crackers that had been pulverized inside her bag over the last two days. Regardless, she didn't have any more food, and she would like to at least keep the little that she had.

She unhooked her white bag and put it on a rock and then leaned herself against another shaded rock. It was midday now, and the sun was bearing down hard upon her head. She was regretting losing her hat earlier. The noonday sun and high elevation were a brutal pair of opponents.

She stared out across the meseta below. It was a beautiful sight, not one that many ordinarily got to see from this height. The plains, yellow and brown, stretched out in every direction.

Her nausea subsiding, Ainsley peered up the path. She could only see about five more switchbacks before the mountain evened out and she lost sight of the trail.

She trudged up the last five switchbacks—

—and finally found herself at the peak of the mountain. It was a flat tabletop, no more than ten meters across. Nearby stood a weathered wooden box on a stand. The breeze caressing her face, Ainsley walked over and noticed that the top was latched. She undid the hasp and pried open the lid.

Inside was an old book. Ainsley knew what this was. She opened the cover and confirmed her suspicions. It was a logbook, full of signatures of hikers. She turned to the last written page and looked at the names. Sure enough, a *Bernadette* and a *Cécile* had signed in today. The name before theirs was Swedish, and it was dated two months earlier.

That was the confirmation she needed. Her quarry were indeed the French women. But where had they gone from here?

She ran to the edge of the tabletop and peered down. The trail continued down a dangerously twisted trail. Off in the distance, she saw the footpath return to the meseta, where it finally evened out and rejoined the Camino. It had become, here on the other side of the mountain range, a double-track gravel road that was clearly visible, even from this distance.

Then Ainsley spotted the French women. The orange and yellow backpacks were tiny blips of color snaking back and forth in the dry brush on the side of the mountain range. If she ran, she could catch them in twenty minutes.

And Ainsley wasn't just a walker—she was a runner. A high school track star who could sprint like a cheetah. True, she was starting to feel an odd twinge here and there, a knee that sometimes felt a little slippy, but these were the wages of age.

She put those thoughts aside, however, as the imaginary starting gun fired in her ear. Without a moment's hesitation, Ainsley bolted off like a shot, high-stepping down the sloped path, feeling the wind at her back and wings on her shoes.

She straddled small gullies in the trail, ran through stands of trees that had been blackened by fire, and crouch-walked beneath low-hanging vines.

A half hour later, she'd emerged from the mountain range a sweaty mess. Her hair was all over her face, her shirt sealed with sweat to her skin, and her mouth hanging open.

The good news was that she'd drawn much closer to the French women now. They looked to be maybe five minutes ahead, straight across the flat meseta. As Ainsley watched, they turned onto the Camino and continued to the west, as if they'd never detoured through the mountains.

Straightaway, Ainsley began running again, across the baked plains, until soon she too was standing in the same place on the Camino, panting like a dog at noon.

Less than two hundred meters ahead, the French women walked on, innocent of the steam engine coming up behind them. In less than two minutes, Ainsley would be alongside the women. Then what would she do? Ask them nicely if she could please look inside their packs? Denounce them for stealing the treasure that she herself had been asked to steal? Then club them over the heads and steal the crystal tiara?

It didn't matter. She would improvise. It had always worked in the past.

Ainsley began to run down the Camino, the last stretch of road between herself and the crystal tiara—

—one hundred meters to go—

—imagining the wealth and fame —

—fifty meters to go—

—arms and legs pumping—

—when she spotted a human being laying on the side of the road. He was on his back in the weeds.

He looked familiar.

Ainsley slowed down and stopped. She turned around. She

went back to the figure on the side of the road and looked down.

It was Graeme.

CHAPTER TWENTY-FOUR

The Scot was stretched out on the ground in the shade of a low shrub. One hand was propped insouciantly behind his head, and the other was tweedling a piece of straw between his teeth.

"You lost your suitcase," he said.

Ainsley was taken aback. "I left it behind."

"Aye, the terrain gets a wee bit tough up in the mountains."

She wondered how he'd known that she'd gone into the mountains. He must've seen her trucking down the trail. Then she studied him. Thirty-six hours earlier, he'd looked like death on a breakfast plate. Now he looked much better.

"I lost my hat, my jewelry, and my tent too."

"That's unfortunate. Did you find the treasure?"

"No, but I think they have it."

"Who?"

She pointed down the trail. "Those French women. They were just ahead of me all the way through the mountains."

He turned his head, then nodded. Ainsley measured her words. "You seem to have recovered nicely, Graeme."

"In a manner of speaking, yes."

"What was the problem?"

He shrugged off. "A passing fever. It was gone by noon. Nothing to be concerned about."

She felt a pang of guilt knife through her torso. "Look, I—"

He waved off her comment before she'd even finished. "Don't bother apologizing."

"But—"

He cut her off. "You don't owe me anything, Miss Walker. You're not walking for spiritual rebirth, you're walking to find something more worldly. So just keep going until you find it."

With visible effort, Graeme pulled himself up to a sitting position. Then he slowly got to his feet. He brushed off the backside of his pants. Then he looked at Ainsley, his eyes filled with pain.

"Why are you still here?"

Ainsley looked down the road. The two figures of the French women were getting smaller. She dandled one foot behind the other, studied her hands, picked sullenly at a cuticle.

"I just ..."

She let the sentence go unfinished. The Scot shook his head in disgust. "You're just what?"

"I don't know."

The Scot began to walk. Ainsley noticed that he was leaning a little more heavily upon his stick.

"You'd better go on ahead," he said. "I'm just going to slow you down."

Ainsley shook her head.

"I'm serious," he said. "Put one shoe in front of the other, and keep doing it, until you catch up to those women."

"I don't want to leave you again."

"Why not? Just walk away. It's your name, isn't it?"

She crossed her arms. "Graeme, I think there's something you're not telling me."

"About what?"

"I don't know. You tell me."

Graeme stood stock still, his jaw jutting out. "You think I have a secret," he said, "and you want to know it."

"Yes."

"Okay, here it is. *I don't care for oatmeal.* See, that's why I was so screwy at the breakfast table."

Ainsley wasn't buying it. "Tell me the truth."

He glared at her but said nothing. Then started hobbling along again. "You don't need to know everything," he said.

She ran alongside him. "Really, I want to know."

"I'm Scottish, Ainsley. We don't spill secrets to the people outside the clan."

"Let me into your clan."

"No."

Ainsley caught him by the arm. "Your mother is dying. You're walking the Camino for her. Why?"

He stopped walking. His eyes fixed wearily upon the horizon, his back stooped under his pack.

"My mother is fine," he said.

Ainsley struggled to understand. "I don't get it. You said that you wouldn't be seeing her for much longer."

He sighed loudly. "You're a bit thick, aren't you? Okay, let me spell it out a bit more directly. My mother isn't the one who's dying."

CHAPTER TWENTY-FIVE

For the rest of the day, Ainsley walked with Graeme on the trail, listening as he narrated the story of his life the last two years. It could be summed up in two words.

Prostate cancer.

He'd been a practicing intellectual property attorney in Glasgow, divorced once, had a daughter he saw every other weekend. Then, age forty-two, during a routine checkup, a doctor's gloved finger had felt something.

An irregularity.

The team of oncologists had recommended exercise as a way to slow the disease. Specifically, they'd told him to exercise like a maniac. It would benefit him to walk as much as possible, as fast as possible, to slow the progression of the disease.

"The only reason they didn't recommend running was the damage that it would do to my knees," he said. "Otherwise I'd be doing a marathon every week."

"You do keep a good pace," said Ainsley.

"It's ironic," he said. "I can only slow down the cancer by walking fast."

She nodded. "So this also explains why you've walked the Camino so many times."

He nodded. "This is my seventh. Have you visited Scotland?"

"No."

"Have you ever walked into a wind tunnel while someone sprayed you with a garden can?"

"Never."

"Try it. That's what hiking in my country is like. I come here to the meseta to dry myself out."

They were bearing across another open field, and Ainsley could see the small figures of the French women about fifteen minutes ahead on the road. She and Graeme had trailed the women all day, but the gap had remained the same, which meant that they were keeping the same pace.

The Scot noticed her. "Don't worry, we'll catch up with them tonight at the *albergue*."

"They stole my tiara," she said.

"It wasn't yours."

"You know what I mean," said Ainsley.

He remained silent for a minute. Then a dark look drew across his face. "I think you'll have to wait longer than tonight."

"Why?"

"Look."

He pointed ahead. Ahead, where the Camino crossed a large four-lane road, a large van had stopped by the side of the road. The French women were climbing inside the vehicle.

"What is that?" she said. "What are they doing?"

"Cheating."

Ainsley's jaw dropped open. "You can't get a *ride* on the Camino."

"People do it all the time."

"But to get the *compostela*—"

"You only have to walk the last one hundred kilometers."

Ainsley felt the anger rising within her. "How far will the van take them?"

"I recognize that van company. They're probably going to skip all the way to Portomarin."

"What's that?"

"It's the last place a *peregrino* can start the trail and still collect the *compostela*. And there's a terrible downhill just before the village, the worst on the entire Frances Way."

Ainsley was indignant. "So they come here, steal the crystal tiara, then cheat their way to the *compostela*?"

He smiled at her wryly. "You were going to steal the crystal tiara too—and you weren't going to finish the Camino either."

She hung her head. Graeme was absolutely right. If she were being honest with herself, she was really no better than the French women. It hurt her to admit it.

"So now what?" she said.

He shrugged. "Me, I'm walking the Camino. It's how I'm going to stay alive. You, I don't know. Maybe you can call a taxi and follow them."

Ainsley watched the van pull away down the road and disappear around a curve. Then she turned to him. "No, I can't do that. I'm going to walk the Camino. And I'm going to do it with you."

He lifted a skeptical eyebrow. "We're ten days away from Santiago."

"I know."

"They're going to be gone by the time that you arrive. You don't want the tiara?"

"Not anymore."

Ainsley was sincere in this. Smiling, Graeme pulled his phone out of his pocket. "That's too bad, because I have the French women's phone number. They made me take it yesterday because they were worried about me. I was going to call them for you."

She stood there in shock. Then a broad grin stretched from ear to ear.

"First," she said, "you persuade me to give up my mission, just to see if I will. Then you turn and give it back to me."

"Aye."

"You are devilish."

CHAPTER TWENTY-SIX

That night, as Ainsley sat back from the dinner table, she realized just how deep her calorie deficit had become.

They were spending the night in a small *albergue* owned by a woman who was renowned for her fantastic meals. True to her reputation, she'd served a sauté of brussel sprouts, cubed bacon, and fava beans, all cooked in sherry and smoked paprika. Ainsley had devoured the concoction, mopped up the juice in the bowl with chunks of hot crusty bread, and washed everything down with three glasses of a local red wine.

It had barely made a dent in her hunger.

Next to her, Graeme had just finished describing to the table one of the sadder stories of the Camino. An old man had lived in an iron bed on the trail for almost three decades. His entire life had been dedicated to helping the *peregrinos*, offering them words, bandages, even the little food or water that he possessed.

"I sat with him on that bed once," he said.

"Why the past tense?" said Ainsley. "Is he dead?"

"He was beaten by local thugs," said Graeme. "They

crushed his chest with tire irons and burned his bed. Now he's in a nursing home somewhere. The bed frame is still there, right on the trail. We'll see it tomorrow."

The other *peregrinos* were a subdued bunch, and as talk turned to more mundane matters, Ainsley excused herself from the table. She walked outside into the darkness, and stuffed her hands into her pockets and lifted her face to the sky.

The moon hadn't risen quite yet, and splattered across the darkness were thousands of pinpricks of light. Maybe it was because they were in the meseta of northern Spain, far removed from any city, but here the stars seemed to shine stronger and truer than anyplace else.

A few minutes later, she heard a door slam. Graeme was walking towards her, a funny smile on his face and a small sack across his shoulder.

"What's up?" she said.

"I called the French women. They're only a day ahead, and they're planning to walk the rest of the way."

Ainsley's eyes bugged out. "Then why did the hell they get picked up by a van?"

The Scot shrugged. "I don't know. Maybe they were tired."

"It doesn't make sense."

"Of course not. But they're women and they're French."

"Hey now—"

He rushed to backtrack. "It's mostly the French, I think. Don't try to understand the French temperament. Many before you have tried and failed."

"Did you ask if they'd found anything in the mountains?" she said.

"Indeed I did," he replied, "but they were very cagey about their little jaunt. No information offered."

Ainsley felt her heart leap in her chest. If these women

had been loath to describe the ladder, the chapel, the women in the petticoats, the narrows, and the waterfall—all of which would make fabulous and exciting stories—then chances were that they were hiding something.

"That is excellent."

He nodded. "I only like to talk about good news."

Ainsley eyed him. "What do you do with the bad news?"

"I stuff it down deep in my soul and wait for it to die."

She laughed, but she couldn't tell if he were being sarcastic. She stared up at the sky again. "Do these stars look any bigger to you?"

"No," he said, "they're pretty much always like this."

"Hm."

He cleared his throat. "There's something else we have to talk about."

"What?"

"Your clothing."

Ainsley looked down at herself—her ripped blouse, her dirty jeans, her hiking shoes. She felt herself growing defensive. "What *about* my clothes?"

"You're going to have to wash them at some point."

That was absolutely true. Ainsley had been so wrapped up in the events of the last two days that she'd forgotten how she'd looked.

"I don't have any other clothing," she said. "I left it all in my suitcase at the base of the mountains. That's two days' behind us."

"True. So I talked to the other diners about your situation, and we took up a collection."

Ainsley lowered her face into her hands. "You're kidding me."

"Don't feel bad about accepting charity," he said. "We all help each other. Here, look."

He reached into the sack and began producing articles of

clothing. A long-sleeved t-shirt. An old windbreaker. Sweatpants. A pair of long underwear.

"That's very thoughtful," she said.

"Aye."

"But most of this stuff is for colder weather. I can't wear it."

"It will get chilly soon."

"All right," she said, "I'll wear some of this, but I'm *not* giving up my coat."

"Positive?"

"Absolutely."

He shrugged. "It's your choice. Now, we get to the last stage of the Camino in two days. It's the place where we rejoin my long-lost Gaelic brethren." He clapped her on the back. "I'll explain more tomorrow, but I'm heading for bed. It's a five o'clock wakeup."

She watched the Scot disappear into the *albergue*. The stars seemed to twinkle a little less brightly after he'd gone.

ASTORGA

CHAPTER TWENTY-SEVEN

Two days later, as Ainsley trudged behind Graeme up a steep slope outside of Astorga, she listened to him describe the Celtic roots of northwestern Spain.

It isn't widely known, he'd said, but the people in this remote corner of Spain are genetically related to the Celts. The theory about the Black Irish descending from the shipwrecked survivors of the Spanish Armada is a great story, but recently geneticists have found that Spanish-Celtic intermingling was going on for centuries before that doomed expedition. Even the Irish Book of Legends features a story of an ancient Galician king who came to rule Ireland.

There's more proof in the cultural traditions as well. The Galicians have long played an instrument known as a *gaita*, which is basically a bagpipe. They have a native dance known as a *muñeira*, which is basically an Irish jig. And one of the most famous Celtic bands in the world, Milladoiro, is from Galicia.

Graeme was eager to share, and Ainsley found herself forgetting to handle him with that special delicacy that she did with the terminally ill.

As they arrived at the top of the windswept hill and crossed a small field, she felt the temperature drop and the wind suddenly pick up. It was time to swallow her pride. She slid the donated windbreaker onto her back, secretly grateful for the charity of the other *peregrinos*.

As they broke out of the field, she saw the most important destination of the day.

An iron cross.

At least ten meters high, it was situated in the middle of a pile of what seemed to be rocks. A small crowd of *peregrinos* were gathered around it, some of them openly praying.

"What is this?"

"The iron cross. You're supposed to leave something here."

She looked more closely. It wasn't just a pile of rocks. It was a pile of rocks, pebbles, bottles, and a thousand other personal bits and bobs. She glimpsed ribbons, scarves, flags, cigarette packs, and wine bottles.

"I don't understand," she said.

"You're supposed to carry a rock in your pocket that signifies the biggest problem in your life," explained Graeme. "After weeks of trekking, you leave it here, on this pile."

"What did you bring?"

He reached inside his coat and withdrew a sheaf of papers. "The latest test results from my radiologist."

"Are they good or bad?"

"Does it matter? It's all I think about."

Ainsley nodded. She watched Graeme slowly approach the pile of offerings, set it down, and place a couple of rocks on top of it. Then he came back.

"I've done that five times now," he said, "but it doesn't seem to be working."

Ainsley wasn't sure what to say to that. Her thoughts

turned to her own offering. Graeme seemed to guess what she was thinking.

"Is there anything that you've been carrying that symbolizes your troubles?" he said.

"Not really."

He rolled his eyes. "Jesus, not that attitude again."

"What do you want me to say?"

"It's okay to be upset, Ainsley."

"No, I'm not upset—"

He grabbed her shoulders and stared into her eyes. "You *are* upset, but it's okay. You're upset because you're learning to look inside yourself."

She stood there, fuming.

"Now let's see what's in your bag," he said.

"Seriously?"

"Yes. Let's see if we can find one object to leave here."

He led her over to an open bench and motioned for her to sit down. Ainsley followed him and then began to empty the contents of her white bag. Her wallet. Passport. Lipstick. Compact. Birth control. Bag of caramels. Cough drops. Face lotion.

Graeme watched impassively. "You see anything that symbolizes your issues?"

Then Ainsley remembered the *abanico de mano*, the one that Joaquim had purchased for her. She unzipped an interior pocket and produced the white fan. Graeme looked at it.

"That's lovely," he said.

"Joaquim bought it for me," she said.

"That was nice of him."

Ainsley felt the tears coming to her eyes. "I was being rude in a store, and he bought it to make peace with the salesgirl."

Graeme seemed to grow calmer. He folded his hands in

his lap and looked out to the horizon. Ainsley felt as though she were in the presence of a yogi.

"Did that argument with the salesgirl contribute to the strength of your relationship?" he said.

"No."

"Did it add any value to your life?"

"No."

The Scot's look said everything. Ainsley knew that this was the item. Drawing a deep breath, she took the *abanico de mano* and walked over to the pile of offerings. She cocked her arm back and threw the item at the pile. It bounced off the iron cross and disappeared down the far side of the stack. She stood there for a moment longer, feeling a sense of lightness.

Then she returned to Graeme. He was tapping the screen on his phone, then stowed it away in his pocket.

"How did that feel?"

She exhaled. "Very good."

"The French women just called me. They're almost at Ponferrada."

"What does that mean?"

"They're two days ahead of us. But I told them that I wasn't feeling well again and they promised to wait half a day for me." He grinned. "I'm going to hell for exploiting my illness."

"You can look me up when you get down there," said Ainsley.

Graeme patted her on her back. "No I won't. And neither will you. We're going someplace else." He hopped to his feet and began walking again.

Ainsley watched him for a minute. If having a terminal illness made someone seem this alive, then maybe she should reconsider what it means to be sick.

CHAPTER TWENTY-EIGHT

For the next seven days, they walked through the final stage of the Camino de Santiago, the northwestern most region of Spain.

Galicia.

They trekked up and down steep hills that were fragrant with pine resin. They cruised down easy paths lined with chestnuts, cherries, peppers, and tall stalks of green fennel. Ainsley learned that on this trail, the Knights Templar once protected pilgrims from bandit attack.

They crouched along remote rivers and ate simple lunches of cured meats and *tetilla*, a strange breast-shaped Galician cheese. Ainsley couldn't ever seem to eat enough. She noticed her pants beginning to slip lower on her waist.

They passed a field in which a thickset shepherd in a knitted cardigan and floppy hat used a stick to swat errant sheep. A little farther on, Ainsley spotted his wife, a gray-haired woman in a dirty apron, standing in the doorway of a cottage. She called off the dogs with a short whistle from two fingers in her mouth.

They accepted homebrewed beer offered by a monk

who'd just finished a long workday in a field of cabbages. Ainsley tasted the sweet ale in the wooden tumbler, and as the monk grew drunker and happier, she kept a safe distance from the razor-sharp scythe dangling from his other hand.

They passed through villages that felt as though they had been dug out of the Irish peat and carried across the water and rebuilt here in northern Spain. She sat at a café late one afternoon with a glass of Albariño, watching an old man carefully braid a Celtic knot.

Her *credencial* grew fuller, with nearly twenty stamps from various *albergues*, restaurants, bars, and grocery stores along the Camino.

On the road, they saw the sky change from blue to rain, to blue again, to rain again—all in less than an hour. Ainsley felt the soft mists cooling her face. She smelled the soft mosses creeping up the stone walls. She heard distant church bells echoing across impossibly lush pastures.

And then, on the seventh day, coming to a crest in a hill, she finally saw the destination.

"That's it," she said, pointing ahead. "Right? Isn't that it?"

Her finger was pointing to a distant hill, on which sat an enormous brown cathedral. A pair of spires poked holes in the low mist.

"Aye," said Graeme, "that's it."

Something about Graeme's voice sounded off. She looked over. The Scot was leaning against a tree, a weird purplish flush spreading across his face.

"You don't look good," she said.

"I'm fine."

"You should rest."

"No," he said, "absolutely not. That's Santiago, right there."

"But—"

"There are no buts," he said. "If I stop walking, I die. Do

you understand? It's like I'm living in that horrible action movie about the hostages on the coach. Except instead of a bomb underneath the vehicle, I've got a poisoned prostate under me, and if I ever stop moving, it's going to blow up."

He straightened himself up, the pain evident in his eyes, his fingers gripping his walking stick. Ainsley could see the sweat springing out on his brow. Her heart went out to him.

"Give me your pack, Graeme," she said.

"Hell no."

"I want to carry it for you. Look, I'm carrying almost nothing."

It was true. For the past week, she'd only been carrying her white bag and the loose sack with her new clothing.

His jaw grew firm in that particularly stubborn Scottish way. "A man carries his own pack, or he's no man at all."

Suddenly one of his knees buckled, and he caught himself on the tree. Ainsley decided that the time for politeness had passed. She walked behind him and pulled the backpack off Graeme's shoulders. He tried to resist.

"Don't fight," she said.

"If I were feeling stronger," he gasped, "you'd be feeling the toe of my shoe up yer arse."

She adjusted the straps, then swung the pack onto her own back. "I'll take a rain check."

"Those are handed out every twenty minutes in this part of the country," he said.

"Stop complaining," she replied, "and let's walk."

For the first time on this entire journey, Ainsley began to take the lead.

SANTIAGO DE COMPOSTELA

CHAPTER TWENTY-NINE

Just outside Santiago de Compostela, Ainsley found herself waiting at a stoplight with nearly a hundred other *peregrinos*.

At this point, the Camino had dwindled to nothing. It wasn't even its own entity, reduced instead to sidewalks marked with the occasional scallop shell marker.

As she stood at the zebra crossing, waiting for the signal to change, she studied her fellow *peregrinos*—the dirty backpacks, the iconic arrows, the dangling scallop shells, the walking sticks, and especially the weary airs of people with an expanded range of vision.

Graeme, however, had continued to decline, and had grown so weak that Ainsley had to occasionally prop him up.

"We'e going to find a hotel," said Ainsley.

Gasping, the Scot tried to be of help. "There's an albergue on Calle—"

"No," she said, "I was talking to the waiter at the café yesterday who recommended that we stay at the *parador*."

His eyes grew wide. "The Parador Hostal Dos Reis Católicos? Next to the cathedral? That's the most luxurious hotel in the country."

She nodded. "You deserve it."

"Maybe you don't understand, but we Scots don't like to pay for places like that."

"Nobody said you were paying," she replied.

Graeme was struck dumb. "Really?"

"Really."

He smiled. "I've always wanted to stay there."

"Good."

Slowly Ainsley helped him through the city, threading her way through the winding medieval cobbled streets. At last they trudged up the final short uphill, and they found themselves deposited in the heart of the city, the Praza do Obradoiro.

Looming above them, as stern as a heavenly judge, was the Cathedral of Santiago de Compostela.

The end of the Camino.

She stood in the middle of the square, near a small marker bearing a scallop shell that had been placed flat amidst the flagstones, and gazed in awe at the cathedral, just as exhausted *peregrinos* have been doing for centuries. To Ainsley, it looked like an incredibly elaborate drip castle at the beach.

"I know you can tell me what I'm looking at," she said.

"After seven visits, I'd better be able to," he said.

He began describing the New Testament story of the tympanum, the sculpture of St. James in the mullion. He pointed out the significant pilasters, the notable archivolts, the grotesque corbels, the hidden jambs. Around the back, he said, was the Porta Santa, also known as the door of forgiveness, which was opened only once a year.

Ainsley began to feel overwhelmed. The cathedral was a lot to take in. Her imagination wandered off to the life of a typical peasant instead. She pictured a medieval grunt—after a day's labor in the field, sitting in rags on a dirt floor, staring into the red embers of a dying fire. She saw the flagon of mead in his grubby fist, sensed his totally empty mind. For that creature, it must have been the experience of a lifetime to see the façade of this cathedral.

"There's a mass for *peregrinos* everyday in the cathedral at noon," said Graeme. "You can find the French women there."

That jolted Ainsley back to the present. The crystal tiara. She'd been so entranced by the cathedral that she'd forgotten the reason she'd come here.

Then she noticed Graeme had fallen silent again. She looked over just as he began to collapse. Shooting an arm around his waist, Ainsley lifted him back to his feet. His head was lolling around again.

"We're getting you to the *parador*," she said. "Where is it?"

His head lolled slowly towards her. His words came slowly from his lips, as though from a distance. "You're ... staring at it ..."

Ainsley looked over. Less than twenty meters away was a long, flat façade of a non-descript stone building. A row of metal stanchions were linked through thick stone pillars before it. Through a pair of glass doors, a doorman awaited them on a red carpet.

"Holy shit," she said.

"It's holy," he said, "but definitely not shit."

Ainsley put her arm around his ribcage and helped him shuffle to the front of the *parador*. The doorman opened the glass door.

"*Peregrinos?*" said the doorman.

"Yeah," said Graeme. "*Numero siete*."

"*Nos falta un cuarto*," added Ainsley.

"*Lo tenemos. Bienvenido*." The doorman held the glass open. Ainsley let Graeme, leaning on his stick, enter the *parador* first.

CHAPTER THIRTY

Later, as she weighed the hair dryer in her hand, the freshly bathed Ainsley felt as though she were experiencing an actual miracle.

Two weeks on the Camino. Two weeks in a cloud of dust and dirt. She'd showered at *albergues*, but only briefly, since most were communal. It hadn't mattered much anyways, not after a few minutes of walking.

The water had turned brown the minute she'd slipped into the bath, so she'd scrubbed herself, then drained the tub and filled it a second time for a more relaxing soak. She'd spent much of the last hour in deep contemplation of her own arms floating at the surface of the sudsy water.

Now, towel around her torso and another around her hair, she heard a knock at the door. Ainsley went back into the suite with its thick medieval walls, tiptoed past Graeme, who was slumbering on his bed in his hiker's clothing, and opened the door.

It was the doorman. He handed her a shopping bag with the name of a fashion boutique on the side.

"Hopefully it is acceptable to you," he said.

"I'm sure it will be," she replied. "I'm not very picky."

Earlier, Ainsley had given him a generous tip, along with a written sheet of instructions regarding what she'd wanted. He'd promised to send someone immediately.

She closed the door and looked down. Inside the bag was a black skirt with an adjustable waist, a green polyester blouse, and a pair of beige flats. It wasn't exactly the most stylish outfit in the world. In fact, it was downright dowdy.

Ainsley didn't care. She was happy for something, anything, new to wear. Her jeans, though expensive, hadn't been designed for the wear and tear of the Camino. She looked at where she'd wadded them up in the corner. They'd seen much better days.

"This is where peregrinos used to die," said Graeme.

It startled her. "Jesus, I didn't know you were awake."

He was laying on his bed, his eyes closed. "Ferdinand and Isabella built this place as a hospital. They used to stack corpses downstairs in the vault." His tongue snaked out and wetted his lips. "It's a fine-dining establishment now."

Ainsley tried not to laugh. "You are *so* macabre."

"We're all going to die," he said. "Some sooner, some later, but we're all headed that way."

"But you're not going to die *here*," replied Ainsley. "Jesus, aren't you happy that you've finished the walk?"

His eyes found hers. "My walking is never going to stop."

Ainsley had nothing to say to that. "I'm going to change for the pilgrims' mass. Why don't you take a shower after I leave?"

"No, I feel weird."

"It's probably the dirt. Take a shower."

"I'll try."

Ainsley went into the bathroom and changed into her new outfit. She looked in the mirror. Something seemed a little different, but it wasn't the outfit. She studied her face.

There were faint laugh lines beginning to form in the delicate skin around her eyes, and her mouth seemed a little less pinched than she'd remembered.

Those weren't bad changes.

When she came out of the bathroom, Graeme was still flat on his back. A light snore was curling out of his mouth.

Ainsley left the room and shut the door.

CHAPTER THIRTY-ONE

At the stroke of noon, Ainsley headed up the front stairway of the cathedral. Just inside the front doors, she entered the vestibule known as the Pórtico da Gloria. A triple portal, it was a three-arched Romanesque masterpiece, the low ceiling rimmed with medieval figures in statuary. She noticed a buck-toothed peasant staring lasciviously at a topless woman.

To the right, she saw *peregrinos* eagerly placing their hands upon a pillar of St. James. This was a centuries-old tradition, according to Graeme, and when they pulled their hands away, she could see the rock had become smooth, shiny, and worn down. That's what centuries of sebaceous glands could do to granite.

Then she moved through the middle arch, into the cathedral proper.

A low whistle escaped her mouth. It was a barrel-vaulted nave, and two rows of massive pillars like the trunks of sequoias ran up and down its length. Two columns of pews, divided by a single aisle, filled the space. At the far end, a priest was standing on the altar, above which rose a golden baldachin, a term she remembered from a long-ago art history class. It was basically a canopy, and this one was a riot of golden decoration. It had enough golden curls to rival a thousand antique French chairs.

Ainsley was surprised to see that the entire cathedral was filled with *peregrinos*. It wasn't any small event. They had crammed into the pews, spilled out into the aisles. Some leaned against the walls, others were too old or too tired or too sick to do anything except sit cross-legged on the floor.

She craned her neck, scanning the crowd—

Then she saw them.

It was the French women. There was no mistaking those two. They were in a pew near the front, on the left. They'd changed clothing, but they still carried the same backpacks, one orange, one yellow.

Ainsley stared at the packs. Inside one of them was the crystal tiara.

She slipped down the left aisle and edged her way through the crowd, moving sideways, ducking slightly, apologizing under her breath, until she was even with them. One of the French women looked over and, seeing Ainsley, gave a little wave. Ainsley waved back, her heart hammering against her chest.

She would confront them after the mass.

Until then, she had to wait.

The event began with the entrance processional. Ainsley stood patiently through the first half of the ceremony, the sprinkling of the holy water, the penitential rite, the Kyrie Eleison, the Gloria, the opening prayer, the first reading, the second reading, the Alleluia, the gospel, the homily, the Nicene creed, the apostles' creed, the prayer of the faithful—

It seemed to go on and on. Shifting her weight, impatiently, Ainsley looked around the cathedral. She noticed, quietly fenced off in front of the altar, a large silver vessel affixed to a thick braided rope that stretched to the dome overhead. It was a beautiful but odd-looking object.

Next came the liturgy of the Eucharist—the preparation of the altar, the prayer over the gifts, the communion rite, the breaking of the bread, the private preparation of the priest. Ainsley sighed, a little too loudly. This mass was seeming to stretch out forever.

When she saw the priest distribute the wafers into the dishes, she knew that it was time to hand out communion. That meant the event was almost finished. Ainsley had taken a communion wafer once before, in Portugal, and had felt uncomfortable, so this time she stayed flat against the wall as the orderly line of *peregrinos* trudged past her with folded hands, waiting to take the body and blood of Christ.

Finally, the Eucharistic portion of the mass ended, and she prepared to confront the French women. She'd been rehearsing her opening line in her head.

To her surprise, the mass wasn't over yet. In fact, she noticed many of the congregants getting pushy, at this point, not to leave, but to get closer to the altar.

To the odd silver vessel.

The priest gave a few words that Ainsley couldn't quite make out, though she sensed that he was telling people not to take any photography. Then he nodded to a team of six men in burgundy robes. They grabbed a circular web of rope to the left of the altar, and in one smooth motion, simultaneously yanked down on it.

The odd silver object was suddenly jerked up into the air.

A hush passed over the crowd.

Next to Ainsley, a man lifted his camera phone into the air, recording the moment. He noticed her watching him. "The *botafumeiro*," he said. "I've waited thirty years to see this."

"It's popular?"

"Of course. Watch when it starts to go."

Ainsley turned her attention back to the object. The men in the burgundy robes began to work the rope in unison. The *botafumeiro* began to swing to the left and right across the transept, slowly at first, then faster and faster. A weird smoke was pouring out from the top of the vessel.

Within a minute it was whistling over the heads of the congregation at an unbelievable speed. The rope was just short enough to prevent it from smashing into either side of the cathedral.

Then a sweet smell reached Ainsley's nostrils, and she realized that the weird smoke was incense.

"You smell that?" said the man.

She nodded. "It's good."

The man grinned. "They started doing it eight hundred years ago because the *peregrinos* smelled so bad when they arrived here." He sniffed his armpit. "Nothing changed."

Eventually the *botafumeiro* slowed down, enough for the men in the burgundy robes to tackle it and guide it back to its fenced-off resting place. The priest gave a final benediction, and the crowd applauded.

The exit procession walked down the aisle, and the crowd began to break. This was the moment. Ainsley turned to the French women, prepared to climb over pews and chase them down.

To her surprise, they walked directly over to her.

"Hello," said one, "where is your friend?"

"They weren't together," reminded the other.

"Graeme is okay," said Ainsley. "He's resting in the *parador*."

"Ah, we stay there too. It's a good place."

Ainsley felt the anxiety building in her ribcage. Her heart felt like it was about to leap out of her chest. "Ladies," said Ainsley, "do you mind if I ask you something?"

"We were going to ask you something too," said one.

Ainsley was taken aback. "What's that?"

The two French women exchanged glances. Ainsley got a prickling feeling at the back of her neck.

"It is a strange question," said one.

"Okay."

The other finished the thought.

"Did you find a crystal tiara on the Camino?"

CHAPTER THIRTY-TWO

Ainsley felt something like a tiny shard of glass catch in her throat. It stayed lodged there, pressing against her vocal cords, making it impossible to speak.

Finally she managed to choke out three words. "You're kidding me."

The French women looked genuinely puzzled. "We are not joking you. Why?"

"I was going to ask *you* if *you*'d found it."

The other *peregrinos* were departing the cathedral now, cutting between them, a flowing river of trekkers, but Ainsley kept her eyes focused on the French women. She was sensing a much bigger story here, and she didn't want to lose it.

"How do you know about the crystal tiara?" said one.

"A priest told me."

They stood agape. "A priest tells to us too!"

"Padre Contrera?"

They both grabbed Ainsley's forearm. "*Oui*!" said one.

"Monsignor Contrera," added the other. "In the confessional at St. Jean Pied de Port."

Ainsley felt even more confused. "No, not there. Contrera was in San Sebastián."

"Was he French?"

"No, he was Spanish."

They released her arms, shaking their heads. "This is a different man. Monsignor Contrera was definitely French."

Ainsley paused to consider the possibility that there could be two priests named Contrera, in two different countries, who were both aware of the existence of a crystal tiara. And that both had sent women in search of this tiara. At the same time.

The chances of that happening were incredibly small.

Then something occurred to Ainsley. "Ladies," she said, "how did Contrera tell you about the tiara?"

"He gave us a poem."

Ainsley dropped her head. She felt the anger starting to rise from her gut like dirty floodwaters.

"Really," she said evenly.

"Yes, he write this poem into our language. It is six lines. I have it." The French woman reached into her pocket and thrust a paper towards her.

Ainsley read the lines. Her *francais* was rusty, but she recognized the words *vert*, *rose*, *mariage*, *larmes*, and *princesse*. It was the same poem, translated into French.

"He gave it to me too," she said, handing it back.

"Then it is a conspiracy."

Ainsley nodded—

—and the French women burst out into fluted laughter, their hands on each other's forearms. "How *fantastique*."

"No," said Ainsley, "it's horrible."

The French women wagged two fingers in the air. "No, not horrible. It's a beautiful, how do you say ... *trick*?"

Ainsley pursed her lips and stared at the floor. Her whole

body felt like it was collapsing. "I walked this Camino for one reason. To find the crystal tiara."

"Now *that* is horrible," said the woman.

"*C'est mal*," echoed the other.

They *tsk-tsked* sadly, then kissed her on either cheek. "Maybe you found something about yourself, no? Is possible?"

Ainsley stared miserably at a spot on the far wall. The cathedral had almost totally emptied out now.

"I have another question," said Ainsley.

"What is it?"

"Did you ever see me walking behind you? When we were in the mountains?"

"Yes, of course," said one.

"We were making fun of you," said the other.

"And you didn't you stop and wait for me?"

The women sneered, and Ainsley felt that famous Parisian attitude rearing its ugly head.

"No, we don't know you," said one.

"We walk together as two," said the other.

"Not three," said the first, wagging her finger. "We are only two."

That didn't make any sense to Ainsley. To her way of thinking, when hiking out in dangerous, remote wilderness, a stranger was a friend, no questions asked.

"Thank you for telling me," said Ainsley.

"*Au revoir*," said one.

"Have a good day," said the other. "Maybe we meet again."

The French women turned and melted away into the cathedral. Ainsley watched them disappear.

Then she was alone, feeling the musty medieval cathedral breathing all around her, as though it were a giant set of lungs that powered the body of humanity. If the world had stopped turning, she wouldn't have cared.

Something caught her eye. It was a wooden box in the far

corner of the transept, beautifully etched, about the size of a photo booth. There were two small doors, each decorated with a thick latticework. A small sign read

Padre Contrera
De 1300 a 1500 horas

Ainsley lifted an eyebrow. There was another Contrera in that little box. Part of her wanted to rip the door off its hinges and pummel whatever impostor sat inside. Another part of her wanted to hand him a cup of tea and find out the real story of the crystal tiara.

Steeling herself, she walked over to the confessional and opened the right door. The confessor's kneeler was empty. She slipped inside and got down on her knees and shut the door. She faced the small wooden screen.

"Padre Contrera," she said.

She waited for the screen to slide open, but there was no response.

"Padre," she repeated.

No answer.

She rapped on the wooden screen with her knuckles. Still nothing. The air started to feel stuffy.

Ainsley opened the door and stepped out of the confessional box. She went to the door on the left and threw it open.

Inside was an empty chair, on which lay a single envelope.

On the envelope was a name. She picked it up and read it.

Ainsley Walker.

She felt her heart leap in her chest. She grabbed the envelope, spun away from the confessional, and ripped it open.

CHAPTER THIRTY-THREE

In the lobby of the *parador*, Ainsley lowered herself onto a couch next to a roaring fire. She began to read the document for the fourth time that afternoon, still trying to process what had just happened.

It was a form letter. Its contents had been written in four different languages—Spanish, French, English, and Korean. Ainsley's eyes went to the English:

Peregrino,

For more than nine centuries, an untold number of people have heard the story of the crystal tiara and undertook the Camino de Santiago. Each of you was tempted to personally find the treasure of the princess, usually because you desired worldly fame, and everything that comes with it.

Like those thousands who came before, you have failed in your task, but perhaps you have succeeded in other ways. And perhaps you understand why the story has persisted.

Look past your disappointment and try to remember that you were born with the treasure of life. Your experience on the Camino has also given you the treasure of self-awareness, of knowledge of God's presence, and the mission to try to be one of God's children. Matthew 23:12 says, "Whoever exalts herself will be humbled, and whoever humbles herself will be exalted."

It is now up to you to keep the secret of the crystal tiara, and to pass along this mission to a person in need of a spiritual journey.

To preserve the secret, please destroy this paper when you have finished reading it.

In God's name,
"Father Contrera"

She stared at the paper, hard enough to make it burst into flames. This had been a joke, a medieval prank, one that had ensnared thousands of other greedy people over the last nine hundred years.

What had it taught her? The practicalities of enduring a very long hike, for sure. How to pop a blister, how to eat like a horse without gaining weight.

It had taught her other things too, but Ainsley wasn't ready to admit it. Not yet.

She balled up the paper and threw it into the fireplace. She watched the orange flames devour the paper.

Then she felt the sudden urge to eat something, have some tea, and then get very drunk. Not the type of emotional drunk where you blubber into someone's shoulder about friendship. Not that dark, smudgy, nihilistic drunk that sends you to sleep facefirst in a puddle of your own vomit. Ainsley just wanted a quiet, deep drunk. A *contemplative* drunk. She wanted to sit in the thick casement of her hotel room, flecks of rain streaking the glass, and stare at the marvel of the cathedral while slowly relieving a wine bottle of its contents.

She wanted Graeme to do it with her too.

Rising to her feet, she saw a nearby waiter carrying a gorgeous cake on a platter. It was a low disk, dusted with powdered sugar, the Cross of St James in the center.

"Excuse me," she said, "what is that?"

"*Es una tarta de Santiago.*"

"Can you send a *tarta de Santiago*, a pot of tea, and a bottle of red wine to my room?"

He nodded. "*Claro.*"

Ainsley gave him the number, then trudged down the stone corridor towards the room. She imagined the thousands of filthy *peregrinos* who had staggered down this very hallway, bleeding from the feet, oozing pustulence, or screaming insane.

Compared with them, Ainsley was doing well. And maybe this, she thought, was the lesson of her journey.

She knocked on the door of her room, just in case Graeme needed to put some pants on. There was no answer. He was probably still asleep.

Ainsley slipped her key into the lock and turned the handle. It popped open. She walked into her suite.

It was empty.

She spun around. A couple of hours ago, Graeme had seemed too tired to move. Now his bed was empty. She looked at the luggage rack where she had laid his backpack.

It was gone.

Ainsley stood in the center of the room, clutching her head. Then she saw the note. It had been laid square on the middle of his pillow, white on white.

She walked over and warily picked it up.

A—

I'm absolute crap at goodbyes, so this will do.

At this point you know that the crystal tiara was an illusion, but even you will admit in time that it's a damn useful one. I searched for it once too.

I appreciate the room, but we Scots don't go in much for luxury, and the road goes ever on for some of us.

And for you too—there's a bit more of the Camino to go. You know what to do when you get there.

We'll meet again. I don't know when or where, but it's something I tell myself whenever I skip out on a goodbye. Think of me often.

—G, the Ancient Mariner

Ainsley read the message twice, both believing it yet not believing it. Graeme had known all along that she was searching for something that didn't exist, but he'd allowed her to make this discovery on her own. She thought about that. People like him, people who didn't judge, people who calmly let you screw up—those were the people you ended up keeping in your life. And it was therefore ironic that he'd walked out of hers. Literally.

There was a knock at the door. She leaped up, hopeful that it was Graeme, that he'd changed his mind and that it'd been a practical joke.

It was the waiter. He was holding a tray bearing an entire *tarta de Santiago*, a pot of tea, and a decanter of red wine.

"Two glasses?" he said.

Ainsley felt a tear in her eye. "No, just one."

FINISTERRE

EPILOGUE

At the end of the Camino de Santiago, Ainsley stared out at the ocean and waited for the police officer to leave.

She knew that he was watching her. He had parked his motorcycle on a nearby turnout and was standing on the lip of the cliff, looking down upon her. She knew that he knew what she was planning to do.

Plunging her hands into her pockets, Ainsley looked back at the expanse of blue saltwater, trying to appear innocent. She thought about all the scallop shells. They had become a symbol of the Camino because medieval *peregrinos* were supposed to bring one back as evidence that they'd visited the ocean. This had been a remarkable accomplishment during a time when people were born, lived, and died without ever leaving their small village.

The police officer checked his watch, then turned and mounted his small motorcycle. He started the motor, kicked out the stand, and slowly drove off down the road.

This was her opportunity.

Ainsley quickly stripped off her coat and dropped it to the ground. With shaking fingers, she unscrewed the cap on the small canister that she'd purchased earlier that morning from a petrol station up the road. She tipped the canister sideways and poured the clear fluid onto the coat, soaking it.

She walked to a nearby trash can and threw the canister away. Then Ainsley produced a moist towelette from her pocket and wiped her hands thoroughly, to get the smell of the gasoline off her fingers. She threw that away too.

There was no time to second-guess. Reaching into her pocket, Ainsley produced a book of matches, stood a fair distance from the coat, struck a match, and tossed it towards the pile. It fell short of the mark and extinguished itself on the asphalt. Ainsley struck another match and watched it suffer the same fate.

Matches wouldn't do. She needed paper.

Ainsley went to her bag and rustled through its contents. At the bottom, she found the original copy of the crystal tiara poem, the one that Padre Contrera—or whatever his real name was—had given her.

Perfect.

She balled up the paper, struck a match, and set it on fire. Then she quickly walked to the coat and dropped the flaming paper onto it.

Ainsley sprang back as the coat instantly caught fire. Within a couple of seconds, a roaring bonfire had sprung up at her feet, scented like gasoline.

As she felt the heat from the fire against her face and hands, Ainsley tried to figure out her feelings. There were many, but she noticed that there was one emotion that she *didn't* feel.

Regret.

That coat had served its purpose, and now it was finished. She'd loved it, but now she could let it go. She pictured her closet, her jewelry drawer, her shoe rack. All of the items in her life that it had once seemed so necessary to own now felt a little less important.

Ainsley stood there for quite a while, thinking about her life on the Camino de Santiago, until she noticed that the bonfire had gone out. She turned her back on the smoldering pile of fabric on the ground and walked up the slope towards the road.

PLOTWORKS PUBLISHING

If you enjoyed this story, please leave a review at the place where you purchased it.

Then visit Plotworks Publishing to follow Ainsley Walker on her next exciting gemstone travel mystery: *The North Korea Onyx*!

Now turn the page for a sneak peek—

THE NORTH KOREA ONYX

Three hours and forty-five minutes after the start of the marathon, Ainsley plunged into the orange tunnel for the fourth and last time.

She was barely jogging at this point. The blisters on her heels felt like gaping wounds, irritating her more with every step. Her legs were long tubes of liquefied butter. The inside of her thighs had begun to chafe severely, despite the promise of anti-chafe pants. She would've traded a week's salary for a finger of petroleum jelly.

The ointment on her scraped cheek had dribbled down the side of her face into the corner of her mouth. It tasted like bitter herbs.

Worst of all, there was a van following about twenty meters behind her.

Ainsley knew why. She'd fallen to the very back of the pack. The organizers of the Mangyongdae Marathon had made it abundantly clear that runners were given four hours to complete the marathon—no more, no less. There was no room for stragglers. She only had fifteen minutes to get back to the stadium.

But she didn't care about finishing the race.

She exited the tunnel and swung around the dogleg for the fourth and final time. Once again, the course opened up, the river to her left, the spectators to her right. The crowd had already thinned out. Many had probably already walked to the stadium for the closing ceremonies.

Her eyes scanned the remaining heads along the barrier. No sign of Kenneth. She hoped that he hadn't been spooked by the previous lap.

With only one more block before the street swung away from the river, Ainsley slowed herself to a walk. She gazed at the faces that watched her curiously. It *couldn't* end like this. She'd travelled too far. Pastor Jeong and his immigrant church had too much on the line.

A swift movement caught her eye. A man had appeared along the barrier at the very end of the block. He stood a head taller than the others.

Kenneth Park.

They locked eyes. Ainsley nodded. He nodded back.

Kenneth leaned over the barrier, as though pretending to get a better view of the runners.

Six steps—

Five steps—

Kenneth held his hand up, his fingers closed upon something.

Four—

Gasping with exertion, Ainsley willed herself to go on.

Three—

She wiped her right palm on her shorts.

Two—

She lifted her right hand and opened her palm.

One—

They locked eyes—

Their hands met—

Kenneth's hand felt cold and soft. In his hand was a hard object. Ainsley closed her palm upon it.

Another stride, and their hands fell apart. She was a step past him, then two steps past, then three.

She felt the item safe in her palm.

Ainsley's eyes grew suddenly bright. Her lungs filled with air. Her heart bloomed in her chest. Energy filled her body.

She'd *done* it. She'd made the exchange. Then she looked down at the object in her hand, and her heart sank.

It wasn't an onyx teacup.

It was a thin canister.

Ainsley's face fell. The tiny plastic container had a cap on one end. It was about the thickness of a pencil and barely as long as her thumb.

Her eyes flamed with anger. The church hadn't contracted her to find a freaking tube of lipstick. What the hell had he *given* to her?

Behind her, an engine gunned. Ainsley glanced backwards over her shoulder. It was the van that had been slowly following her.

It was speeding up.

Shit.

The driver had seen the exchange.

Ainsley didn't have any more time to worry about the contents of the canister. She had to worry about keeping it. She quickly stuffed it into her bra, praying that her meager endowment would keep it safe.

Straight ahead was a sign with lettering in Korean. Underneath was the word *Rest station*. She scanned the area. Card tables with tiny cups of water. Garbage cans overflowing with crumpled cups. Staffers sweeping the ground with a wide broom.

Then she saw the port-a-potty.

Perfect. She would open the canister there. In private.

Ainsley angled off the racecourse and walked to the toilet. There was no line. As she reached for the handle—

—a man's hand grabbed her forearm and yanked it back. Startled, Ainsley looked at him. It was a member of the race staff. He wore an intimidating scowl on his face.

"No," he said.

"I go here," she replied, tapping on the bathroom door.

"No," he said, then gestured back to the course. She looked back and saw the van stopped, waiting. Another man stood by the door, hand on the handle.

"There?" she said.

His words came at her like a spray of bullets. "You go there. Ameri-*can*."

She noted the extra spite dripping from that last syllable. "Into the van?"

"You go *there*."

His hands pushed at her as if kneading a blob of dough, until she found herself stumbling towards the van. Was she being arrested? Detained? Deported?

She dropped her hands to her sides, a sign of nonresistance. At the van, the man slid open the door. Inside were seven other runners, looking utterly spent. Ainsley quickly sussed out the situation. These were the slowpokes. She was being rounded up to be taken to the stadium for the closing ceremonies. Apparently people weren't allowed to finish at their own pace.

She turned to the staffer. "But the stadium is right there. I can finish in ten minutes."

The race staffer's hands chopped and pushed at her back, pushing Ainsley into the van. "You go *there*."

Reluctantly, she climbed inside with the other runners. Then the door slid shut and the van began to move. Ainsley felt the canister growing warmer against her heart.

They arrived at the gate of the stadium, and Ainsley slowly disgorged from the vehicle. She began to limp towards the stadium entrance. Two minutes of sitting, and her legs had already begun to cramp.

She passed through the opening—

—and emerged onto the broad track that circled the floor of the stadium. Strange orchestral music floated out of unseen speakers. To her left was the finish line, but she needed to run one more lap to arrive at it.

In the middle of the field, behind a rail, were the other runners, nearly two thousand. Some were standing and chatting, sipping from cups. Others had flopped backwards onto the floor of the stadium. A few were being tended to by paramedics.

Towering all around her in the stadium seats sat one hundred and fifty thousand spectators. As she summoned all her strength to begin running the final lap, she felt the hair on her neck stood on end. The eyes of the entire stadium were upon her at that moment.

The small canister sizzled against her ribcage like a burning secret.

A minute and a half later, she crossed the finish line, barely noticing. Then she was allowed into the field proper, with the other runners. Someone handed her a towel. Another person handed her a large cup of water.

Ainsley moved through the crowd as though in a dream. They were milling about, laying on the ground, doing jumping jacks, laughing, crying. The scent of body odor was strong, even in the cool air. A few were even asleep on the ground.

Ainsley ignored all of them. All she wanted was twenty seconds of privacy to open the canister.

She found a row of portable toilets. The line was stacked twenty deep.

Forget it.

Ainsley finally sat down on the ground and draped the towel over her head. It was dark in here. Nothing but the sensation of her own breath, the chatter of the people around her, the distant lilting violins from the loudspeakers.

Nobody could see her.

She reached into her bra and pulled out the canister. Careful to keep it concealed under the towel, she popped open the cap and tilted the canister upside down.

Nothing came out.

She reached her pinky finger inside and slowly drew it out.

A slip of paper.

She heard a roar go up from the crowd outside the towel. She heard the sound of exploding fireworks outside the stadium.

Ignoring the commotion outside, Ainsley unrolled the small slip of paper with trembling fingers. On it was a scrawled message.

It was too dark to read beneath the towel, so she pulled it off her head. A riot of red-and-white fireworks exploded in a ring around the stadium. At the gate, a large military procession had entered and begun to march around the track.

Ignoring the ruckus, Ainsley looked down at the note in her hands. She read the words.

She couldn't believe what it said, so she read them a second, then a third, time.

Run to the market. They're coming for you.

PLOTWORKS PUBLISHING

Visit Plotworks Publishing to follow Ainsley Walker on her next exciting gemstone travel mystery!

Then explore a new series by J.A. Jernay—the Cosmo Bennett Mapping Thrillers!

Turn the page for another sneak peek—

BOUNDARY

Cosmo and his assistant Noah shuffled down the dirt shoulder of the boulevard in the midday heat, sweating and miserable.

Each was lost in his own thoughts. Cosmo dreamed of hitting a heavy punching bag at his gymnasium. Noah dreamed of passing level nineteen of Operation Earlobe, an obscure RPG he'd abandoned last semester.

The morning's meeting had been a complete bust.

"I don't think we should continue," said Cosmo finally.

Noah didn't respond, but Cosmo took no notice. He continued: "I don't think anybody here takes our task seriously. I don't think this propaganda map was as influential as they say. I don't think this map has driven the civil unrest. I think social media and centuries of tribal warfare are more to blame for the unrest than anything else."

He looked over at Noah, waiting for a response. "What about you?"

The graduate assistant came back from his reverie. "Huh?"

"Did you hear anything I said?"

"No."

"I was just saying this is pointless and we should go home."

"I don't have a problem with that."

They arrived at Vida e Caffe. It was a chain café, with hundreds of similar franchises scattered across the southern half of the African continent. The branding was modern and inviting. A hundred people sat beneath umbrellas at small tables on the large outdoor patio.

An arm was waving at them. It was Christopher, their fixer, a cup of tea on a ceramic saucer in front of him. Two other cups awaited them.

"Hello sirs," he said. "I ordered us all a rooibos. It's a vanilla tea that is extraordinary."

Cosmo and Noah pulled out the chairs and sat down. The driver quickly sussed out that something was wrong.

"It was a bad meeting?" he said quietly.

"Yes," said Cosmo, "there was no progress made."

"I'm very sorry."

Cosmo sighed. "I think we have to leave."

The fixer looked confused. "But you just sat down—"

"The country," he clarified. "We have to leave Fabajouti. We can't seem to do any good here."

Christopher looked crestfallen. "I do understand your frustration."

Noah said, "If it's okay with you, we'd probably like to just get in the car and go back to the hotel."

The fixer rediscovered his manners. "Of course, as you wish—"

"But we'd love to try the tea first—" added Cosmo.

"You two enjoy the rooibos," said Christopher, "while I fetch the car. The parking lot is very jammed and it will take quite a while to remove. I've already paid the bill."

Before they could object, the driver had shot to his feet.

He clapped Cosmo on the shoulder and left the patio. They watched him cross the boulevard to an off-street parking area that was crammed tightly with vehicles. On his approach, the attendant began shifting other vehicles.

Noah sipped the tea. "This does taste really good. I don't drink enough tea."

"I like tea," said Cosmo. He sipped from the cup. "This one is good."

"What's your favorite?" asked Noah.

"Maybe pu'er."

"That one's bitter, right?"

"Yeah. It's fermented."

"What about Earl Grey?"

"A cliché."

"I think I'm more of a fruity tea guy," said Noah.

Cosmo nodded. "Yeah, they have their charms."

"You ever try chamomile?"

"It's good for sleeping," said Cosmo, "but otherwise it's—"

His comment was cut short by a massive fireball that erupted from the parking lot across the street.

In a split second, Cosmo and Noah instinctively rolled off their chairs and onto the ground beneath their table. Their eyes met. Each was filled with terror.

Then the shock of the overpressure hit. Cosmo felt the force of the blast wave hit the left side of his body. The highly compressed air rattled the left side of his skull. It even sent his lips and cheeks flapping to the right.

The initial sound of the explosion was deafening, but that was soon replaced by a symphony of falling destruction. A thousand pieces of metal, plastic, glass, and upholstery rained down upon the boulevard, the grass, the other cars.

A shower of tiny shrapnel hit on the patio of the cafe. One hit Noah in the hand and sizzled his flesh. He shook it off.

They waited another few seconds for the shrapnel rain to end. Then Cosmo and Noah lifted their heads.

The patio of the café was transformed into pandemonium. The patrons started to pull themselves up from the ground and flee out to the street and in the opposite direction. The street itself was coming alive with panicked people running in every direction.

"What the actual—" said Noah.

"Christopher!" interrupted Cosmo. "What about Christopher?"

He scrambled up to his feet. Without waiting for Noah, he sprinted out of the café and across the boulevard, weaving through the stopped cars. The air was acrid with chemicals and the heat had somehow intensified even further.

The parking lot was a field of wreckage. The bomb had exploded in the middle of the space, shredding every vehicle and person within twenty meters. Pieces of concrete and metal and glass had been blown across the scene.

"Christopher!" he shouted again. "Christopher! Don't do this!"

He saw a shoe with a foot still in it. He saw a red string of guts entangled in a hubcap. A wave of nausea gripped his stomach. He covered his nose with his t-shirt and backed away.

He tripped backwards over a piece of metal, stumbled, and fell to the ground.

That's when he saw it.

A long strip of shredded fabric. A yellow-and-green printed tropical shirt.

It was bloody and torn.

Cosmo turned his head and retched onto the asphalt. All the tea he'd just drank came out.

He somehow pulled himself to his feet and staggered back to the café. Noah was waiting at the far corner, on the sidewalk, pacing frantically.

"So?"

"I found him," said Cosmo. He forced the next words out. "A little bit."

Noah's face went white. "Oh my God."

Cosmo didn't say anything. He just gripped Noah by the upper arm. "Walk with me. And don't look back."

The pair moved briskly down the boulevard, away from the scene. People were running past them, mouths open, eyes full of fear, but Cosmo maintained a steady pace. His face betrayed an intense desire to appear as normal as possible.

"So we're just going to leave the scene?" said Noah.

"Yep."

"Why?"

"Don't make me answer that, Noah."

"I think we should talk to the police, cooperate, tell them everything—"

"In a different country," Cosmo replied, "in a different scenario, you'd be right. But not here, not now."

Noah looked back over his shoulder at the scene.

"Look straight ahead," Cosmo said through his teeth, "and listen to me. Our Mercedes is gone. Christopher is ... gone."

"Shit—"

"And I'm going to suggest something else that could blow your mind."

"What?"

"It's possible that we were the intended target."

"That's insane."

"Is it?"

"How do you know?"

"I don't. But it's a possibility. Here's another one. It's possible that we are going to be used as scapegoats. We were the last people seen eating with Christopher. Do you want to be put in a Fabajouti jail on suspicion of a crime?"

They walked for another half minute in silence. Behind them, the chaos grew distant.

"Where are we going?" Noah said finally.

"Back to the hotel."

"And then?"

"We're leaving, like we planned."

"We're not going home, are we?" said Noah.

Cosmo's mouth grew hard and his jaw jutted out. He stared straight forward at an invisible point on the horizon. "No, we're not."

PLOTWORKS PUBLISHING

Visit Plotworks Publishing today for all these titles—and more!

www.ingramcontent.com/pod-product-compliance
Lightning Source LLC
LaVergne TN
LVHW051002080826
845145LV00009B/2410

* 9 7 8 1 9 6 0 9 3 6 2 4 0 *